K WEBSTER
J.D. HOLLYFIELD

Dedication

This book is dedicated to the two cutest and funniest gals we know…*us.*

Dear Reader,

We hope you enjoy our cute romantic story! The two of us had an absolute blast writing together. One of us took the hero's POV and the other took the heroine's POV so have fun trying to decide who wrote what. The answer is in the back...no cheating!

This book was nothing but laughter and fun on our end so we hope that you can feel that as you read along.

It's time to sit back and enjoy this funny, sweet ride. We hope you love reading it as much as we loved writing it!

See you on the flip side!
K Webster and J.D. Hollyfield

"You do not find love. It finds you."
—*Suzy Kassem, Rise Up and Salute the Sun: The Writings of Suzy Kassem*

Chapter One

Dani

> ### The Start of Nothing Good

"THAT TWO-TIMING, LOW LIFE, SON OF A BITCH," Andie, my best friend since grade school, yells while I take the double shot of tequila she insisted I drink and slam it. The burn traveling down my throat causes my eyes to water, but I raise my hand and wave down the bartender to get a refill.

"Dani, I swear it, girl. I told you to dump his sorry ass a long time ago. I knew he wasn't doin' you right."

I turn to her and nod my response. Because I'm fighting not to cry and if I try speaking, I will most definitely break down and do so.

"Honey, say something. You haven't said a word in the last thirty minutes, and it's starting to worry me."

And being worried is a fair assessment.

"More tequila, please," I say, my voice quivering. I

can't believe Daryl did this to me.

Thirty-seven minutes ago, I walked—more like got dragged by Andie—into Bender's Bar, a local hangout in our small town of Bensenville, North Carolina because Andie got a tipoff from a girlfriend, which led to me catching my cheating jerk of a boyfriend with his so-called neighbor. And I'm sure you can figure out that they were doing way more than being *just* neighborly. Catching him with his tongue down her throat was the first sign that I was right. He was a cheating jerk, but the closer I got, the better I was able to see the second sign: the shiny new ring on her finger that was practically blinding me.

Thirty-five minutes ago, I set the record for how fast a girl could make a guy scream for mercy. Because I beat the living crap out of him. *Okay, so I take that back. I* just stood there in shock. Andie, the one with the backbone and stiff tongue of our friendship, did the honors for me. While I stood there like the polite person I was raised to be, staring at my boyfriend, with Stacey, his "we're just friends" neighbor, Andie yelled and called him every low-life name in the book.

Every few purse whacks, I attempted to open my mouth and say something, but then that ring would flash in my peripheral vision and I would lose my backbone to fight. Because not only was he cheating on me, he apparently just proposed as well.

And I know what you're all thinking. This is for the best. Once a cheater, always a cheater. Get rid of him. And I would also say that I agree. Daryl had to go. I may have loved him, but he was no good. So I did what any girl would do and avenged my honor—in my head of course—because with the way I was raised, I couldn't be rude to a fly. Having spent my entire life hiding behind my timid shell, I allowed him to choose his new *fiancée* over me.

He didn't try and plead with me that I saw it all wrong. Knowing me, he could have told me she was choking and he was just offering her CPR and I would have believed him. Because that's the person I am. The one everyone takes advantage of. But no, with the help of a bouncer, he escorted his future bride out. That future bride *not* being me. And as he passed me, he told me we were over and to never contact him again.

You know what I said? "Oh, um, okay…"

Nearly a year of my life of devotion, and *poof!* Gone.

I would have said more, but Andie was taking center stage, tossing salt and pepper shakers at his back, yelling things her mother would keel over in her grave about if she heard come out of her mouth. The second the door shut behind them, Andie was grabbing my phone and deleting his number.

"He won't have to worry about you calling him, that two pump, no good cheating asshole!" She handed me back my phone, and I numbly took it, with one thought in mind. Just last week he convinced me to fork up most of my savings for a loan he needed help on. Yeah. I just gave my cheating, now ex-boyfriend his down payment, which I'm pretty sure went to that ring.

God, I'm such an idiot.

"Another round! Come on! We're dying of soberness here!" Andie yells across the bar to the tattooed brute working behind the counter. "I swear, we should go find him and egg his car. No wait, bologna his car. I hear that takes the paint off."

I should be agreeing with her, trying to muster up any sort of revenge, but I can't. I'm sitting here numbly thinking that would not be nice, and I would feel bad for ruining his car. *God, when did I become such a pushover?*

The bartender finally looks our way and his eyes catch mine. The way he's staring me down makes me uncomfortable. Maybe it's because he looks like he wants to eat me. But not in a good way. More like eat me up and spit me out.

He makes his way over to us. "Since my only job is to service you two ladies, what can I get ya?" He wipes his hands off on a bar towel, tossing it over his shoulder. I notice his thick arms, covered in a colorful array of tattoos. His hair is dark and pulled back into a ponytail as he stretches his arms across his chest.

"I'm so sorry, you're right. Please, whenever you're ready, we would—"

Andie cuts me off. "No, fuck that. Yes, we would like two more double shots of tequila, chilled, pronto," she demands and then slaps her hand on the bar.

My eyes widen at her bold delivery. I turn to the bartender. "I'm sorry. Please just whenever—"

"DANI! For real! Stop being so fucking nice."

"I'm just being polite. He's kind enough to serve—"

"Oh my God! Dani, it's his job to serve us." She pauses to make eye contact with the bartender. "No offense," she says, turning back to me. "See, this is why people take advantage of you. You're too damn nice."

"I am not," I lie because I've been told how nice I am

my whole life. *Can you let my dogs out, cover my shift, pick up the bill? Thanks, you're so nice…*

"Dani, listen. Daryl's an asshole. You did everything for him, and he still cheated on you. With his *neighbor*." Her words are harsh, but true. I did do everything for him. Cleaned his condo. Picked up his dry cleaning. Cooked his *neighbor* food while she was sick and he was out of town on business. "You *need* to stop letting people walk all over you. You *need* to start standing up for yourself."

Not realizing the bartender left, I'm startled when he returns, placing two shot glasses in front of us.

"I don't think I should drink anymore," I start to say, but Andie sticks her hand over my mouth.

"You need to do just that. Fuck him. Let it out, girl. I know you're upset. I also know you're trying to be nice and probably wondering if he still needs his shirts pressed for Monday!"

My lower lip begins to quiver, because I was thinking just that. "He has important staff meetings on Mondays and it's critical he looks—"

"STOP!"

I jump out of my seat. I turn to Andie, who is pushing the shot glass into my hand. "Take this, or I call your mother and tell her you had a boy in your room in high school and he almost got to second base under her roof."

Oh my God…she wouldn't.

"If you're asking whether or not I'd do it, then the answer is yes I would. Now drink." She clinks my glass, swishing the liquid.

My parents were very religious when I was growing up and if they had their way, I'd be ninety before allowing

5

a boy to hold my hand. So needless to say, my sexual experiences and dating record was miniscule. If it wasn't for Andie and her sweet scandalous smile, my parents probably would have never believed we were studying at her house instead of at the high school keg parties. Which I didn't drink at. Because I wasn't twenty-one.

"Okay, oh my God. I'm not calling your mother. But take it now!"

With a groan, I throw the shot back, letting the liquid once again burn. The taste is something that belongs in a gas tank, not a human body.

I start to choke on the aftertaste, when the bartender hands me a lime. "Suck on this," he says. Looking back at him confused, I see Andie already shoving it in her mouth, so I follow suit. The citrus assault mocks the burn and actually dilutes the awful taste.

"Than—Thank you," I reply, picking up a napkin and wiping my lips. When I grab for my wallet, he sticks his hand up and shakes his head.

"Nah, it's on the house. Sounds like you deserve it."

"I couldn't possibly accept—"

"Your friend's right. You're too nice. You need to toughen up."

My mouth drops open. Even a complete stranger is telling me I'm a total pushover.

"Some guy do you wrong?" he questions, his face hardening a bit.

Did he ever...

"Her cheating asshole of a boyfriend just got caught, and not only did he get caught but proposed to another girl!" Andie shouts in disgust.

Gee, thanks, best friend. Now I look like a complete fool to this stranger.

"That why you look like your puppy just died?" He wears a look of pity.

I bring my hands to my face. "I do not look like that…"

"Babe, you look sad as shit. Besides the flush in your cheeks from the tequila."

I do feel a little warmer. I admit, I don't ever drink. It was just another thing my parents frowned upon. I bring my eyes back to the bartender, and with renewed boldness I ask, "What would you do if you were me?"

His lips draw up on one side while mischief flickers in his eyes. "Babe, a good lookin' gal like yourself? I'd get even."

I gasp. Get even? "I don't even know what that means."

The bartender leans forward, his large frame close. Andie and I both lean toward him as if he's about to tell us a huge secret. "Get mean. Get ugly. Tell him you've had better, already gettin' better. Shit, send him pics of your tits, tell him he ain't gonna ever suck on those fine ass nips again." We both gasp at his words.

"God, that's a great idea," Andie sighs, while I punch her in her side, gently of course. Hard would be rude.

"I *cannot* do that."

"Yes, you can." That's Andie *and* the bartender in unison.

I look to the bartender and he's lifting a bottle above the bar, refilling our shots. "You can do it. I'll help give you the courage, darlin'."

I tell them both I can't. That's just not me. I would prefer to lick my wounds in private and move on. Daryl cheated on me. He felt our eight-month relationship wasn't good enough, so he had to dishonor me, and what we had. And then use me and my kindness to sucker me into loaning him almost ten thousand dollars.

It's strange how alcohol really does fuel the anger secretly living inside us all. I begin to think about all the things I wanted to do with that money. How hard I saved. All the trips, lunches, and clothes I passed on so I could put that extra money in my savings. Gone, all because some no-good jerk scammed me and bought his new girlfriend a ring.

"Uh oh, she's getting quiet again. Earth to Dani…"

"I paid for that ring," I blurt out, the liquor kicking in. I turn to Andie, then to our new friend. "The neighbor. Her ring. My money."

"What do you mean *your* money?" That's Andie.

"My money. Daryl asked me last week to loan him ten thousand dollars. And I did." Andie's mouth drops so far down, I feel it would only be the nice thing to do and pick it up. I reach out, shutting her mouth for her and turn to our friend. "True story," I say as I nod, and accidentally burp. Ew!

"That son of a bitch! He is *not* getting away with this," my best friend growls.

"Well, he kinda already has. And looks like she said yes." I giggle, covering my mouth, shocked at my out-of-nowhere humor.

"Dani, give me your phone." She reaches out and grabs it before I even offer it to her. Scrolling through my contacts, she mutters, "Shit, what's his number? I forgot I deleted his ass."

"Why?" I question. "What are you going to do?"

"I'm going to text him and tell him what a small fucking penis he has and that you hope it falls off or that he gets attacked by a wild bear who rips his legs off." I don't know why, but I start laughing. Like hard. What's wrong with me? The tequila has definitely kicked in. I grab for my phone and fumble with it, trying to get it unlocked.

"Listen, this is my problem. I'll text him." I open up the phone and go into my contacts. I go to dial his number. *1-555-657-43...* No, that's not it. *Backspace.* *1-555-657-53....* No. Shoot, that's not it. *Backspace...*

"Dude, you okay?"

"Yeah, I just... just didn't have his number memorized. I'm trying to... Oh wait! I know. *One, five five five, six five seven, five three four three.* There! That's him. Daryl Winston. Cheating jerk of the century." I smile, looking at my audience. "Now, what do I say?"

I sit there for a solid five minutes listening to them both shoot out ideas. All words that they should be ashamed of having come out of their mouths. I never understood the whole, let's-get-vulgar talk. Strangely, though, they're convincing me that it is one hundred percent the way to go.

"Okay, so this sounds okay, right?" I put my phone up to my eyeballs because it's easier to read this way. "You ass sucking motherfucker." I can't go any further without laughing. My mother would wash my mouth out with soap if she heard me. "Okay, okay, sorry. You ass sucking motherfucker, you made a big mistake today. No one breaks up with me."

They both take it in, their thinking faces in full effect.

"I mean it's *good*," Andie says, tapping her chin with her finger. "Could be better, but oh well, send it."

I turn to Brett, who we learned during our conversation was the bartender's name.

"Short and sweet, babe. Send it."

I nod to them both and without another thought, I press SEND.

And then I panic, grabbing for my phone, hoping it was a bad dream and I really didn't just send such a horrible message to my ex. I feel like I'm going to be sick. This is not me. I may be hurt and he may have just royally taken advantage of me, my kindness, and my heart, but it doesn't give me the right to lower myself to his standards.

I put my phone down, waiting for the hurtful response I'm going to get. Five minutes pass, then ten, and still nothing. After everything I gave him, he can't even respond to a text message? My legs begin to tap under the bar, and I'm feeling anger brewing in my belly encouraged by the fearless new inhabitant named Tequila. Brett pours another shot, and although I know I don't need any more, I take it.

"How dare he?" I demand, picking up my phone and typing in one of the many messages we rehearsed.

Me: You were horrible in bed. I get more pleasure fingering myself than with your small dick.

"There's no way he won't reply to that one." But another five minutes goes by and nothing. My anger is getting the best of me, and before I know it, I'm shooting off message after message like a madwoman.

Me: You suck cock and I'm telling everyone.

Me: Man, your hairline is so far back, archaeologists couldn't find it.

Andie snorts over my shoulder.

Me: Jump off a bridge you fat fucker.

By the last text message, I've lost all grasp on reality, and get the hint that he isn't going to reply. I make sure to resave his contact so I don't forget it again. As the tequila swishes in my belly, I text him one last drunken time:

Me: My name is Inigo Montoya! You killed my father! Prepare to die.

Ding.

Cheating Asshole: Did you just quote *The Princess Bride*?

"OH MY GOD!" I yell. "He finally messages me back and THIS is what he replies with?" Andie grabs my phone from my hands and reads the message. "What the fuck?"

"I know!"

"No, I mean what the fuck does that mean? You typed a quote from a movie?"

I mean, well yeah. Why not? "Seemed fitting," I say.

"Oh well, we have his attention. Keep going."

Taking my phone back, I go in order of the questions we went over.

Me: Why is your dick so small and useless?

Cheating Asshole: I don't think it's small at all. I've always been voted top in my class.

What a conceited ass!

11

Me: Well, it did nothing for me.

Cheating Asshole: Maybe it's because I would have had to be present to use it on you.

Oh, now he's acting like he was never mentally there when we had sex?! The nerve!

Me: Your taint smells like horseshit.

That text was brought to you by Andie who snatched my phone from my hands.

Cheating Asshole: Maybe you should come over and offer me a redo.

When hell freezes over. My vulgar mouth seems to have taken over. This unfamiliar person who has taken over my body starts typing the next message before even consulting with me.

Me: No thanks, and for the record, I suck great dick. You're going to regret breaking up with me.

Cheating Asshole: Sounds like you do. Again, come over. Put your mouth where your words are.

Just as I'm typing my rebuttal, another text comes through. Pulling the phone closer, I read the message from another number. That number being *1-555-657-5363*.

1-555-657-5363: I want the key you have to my place back.

It takes a few seconds for it to register. And when it does, I freeze.

"Holy shit." I stare at my phone. I go back to the number I've been texting. And then back to the number that just came through. Not Daryl, and then Daryl.

Text 2 Lovers

"Oh my God! I typed in the wrong number!"

"What?" Andie yelps, leaning over looking at my screen. "Well, then who the hell have we been talking to?"

Chapter Two

Ram

> **As You Wish**

THE PRINCESS BRIDE. SOMETIMES INSPIRATION strikes in the simplest of ways. Last night, after getting an accidental reaming by a stranger and having her—I'm assuming it was a *her*—quote *The Princess Bride*, a mental block in my head was obliterated. I've been staring at my computer for weeks in an attempt to come up with an entire branding package for a client. Websites are usually my forte and where I start—at least that's how I did it at my old job. I build the logo, slogan, and brand from there. But for my first potential client on my own, I was coming up short. After the sad, drunk girl most likely fell asleep, since the texts were no longer coming in, I sat up all night designing Inigo Photog's website.

Inigo.

The name hadn't had any meaning to me until she quoted his character from the famed 80's movie. *Of course* it made perfect sense to build a theme around *The Princess Bride* movie. I worked through the night and by dawn, I had something to send to the client. Finally. I'm just stretching and standing to seek out coffee when my phone buzzes.

> **Buttercup: I am SO sorry. I texted you by mistake. I'll erase your number and you'll never hear from me or my terrible friend Tequila ever again.**

Of course I saved the sad stranger's name as Buttercup. The name of the heroine from the movie. I smirk at her text before sauntering out of my bedroom in the loft I share with my older brother, Roman. As soon as I exit my room, I smell coffee. Thank God.

> **Me: Sounds like that asshole deserved it. Did you ever forward on those colorful insults or were they for my privilege only?**

I'm grinning when I enter the kitchen.

"Are you sick, Ram?" my brother's deep voice questions.

I glance up to see him already dressed for the office. He dons a three-piece suit and a permanent scowl. At one time he was my boss. That is, until *his* boss made him fire his own brother. Things haven't been exactly kosher lately.

"I'm fine," I grunt as I snag a mug from the cabinet. "Why?"

He sips his coffee and his eyes narrow. "Well, for one, I haven't seen you roll out of bed before eight in four months."

The reminder of how long I've been unemployed while desperately making a stab at being self-employed and relying on my brother to pick up my part of the rent stings.

"You know I can't sleep," I snap. Truth is, I've developed an annoying case of insomnia—*again*—ever since I was fired in such a humiliating way. I keep replaying how the CEO stood by with everyone in the company looking on as he waited for my brother to let me go. All over some stupid bullshit. My then girlfriend at the time, Chelsea, even had the gall to look disgusted. It pisses me off that she didn't back me up.

"Yeah, I hear your annoying chair creaking as you swivel back and forth all night. Most people sleep at night because they actually get *into* their bed," he grumbles and takes another sip.

I simply shrug as I pour some coffee into my mug and dump an unhealthy amount of sugar into it. "Do you want me to move out?"

His gaze softens and he tugs at the knot on his tie. My brother. A stiff suit. I'd attempted to follow in his footsteps, even accepted the marketing job at his company he worked at, but I was never good at working for the man. Where Roman has always been the rule follower, I've always been one to color outside the lines.

"You're not moving out, asshole," he replies, a small smile tugging one corner of his lips. "I'm just shocked is all. What's gotten you out of bed and looking more like my brother this morning? Did you land that client?"

I see the hope in his eyes and it wounds me. Ever since I was let go, he's encouraged me to start my own marketing company. One where I'm the only employee. I liked the idea, but it's been harder than I thought. Companies are pretty loyal to the people they currently use. And convincing them to reevaluate their branding takes a lot of unpaid work on my end because I have to show them the potential. It's slow going, but the idea of working for myself is actually quite exciting.

"I was stuck on a design concept but I finally worked through it. If I land Inigo Photog, that'll get me my start," I tell him, my voice low.

He slaps my shoulder and grins. "Best news I've heard in a long time. Want to meet me for lunch today? We could go have some beer and wings at that tavern we used to always go to." Again, another hopeful look in my older brother's eyes. I suppose I have been sort of a grumpy ass the past four months. My brother and I used to do everything together. After I was let go, I'd slipped into a depression—*again*—where I slept all day and obsessed over my life's direction at night. It didn't leave much time for watching football with my brother like we used to or occasional lunches where he'd hit on the waitresses, much to my amusement.

"Lunch sounds good," I agree. "But I'm not coming up to the office. Meet me at the tavern."

A dark look passes over his features. "I'd never ask you to go back there. Not after what happened."

Relief floods through me, and I tip my chin at him. "Speaking of. Don't you need to get out of here?"

His gaze darts to his watch and he groans. "Fuck. I'm going to be late." As he passes me, he slaps my shoulder again. "Noon." He flashes me a wide grin that reminds me of our deceased father's. "Glad to have you back, man."

After Roman leaves, I settle back at my desk with a fresh cup of coffee. My mind is buzzing with ideas for this branding package. It's the best I've felt about a design since before the big spectacle.

Anger ripples through me. They never even investigated. Never even gave me a chance to explain that I'd received the email from Chelsea, daughter of the CEO James Tucker, and my then girlfriend. That it was a virus. At least I'd hoped. Surely she wouldn't send that shit to me on purpose.

But I can't forget the look of contempt in her eyes. My uptight Chelsea no longer looked at me like I was her shiny new toy. The spoiled brat clearly got tired of me and discarded me as if I were nothing.

And by discarded, I mean sent me a goddamned kiddie porn virus.

I shudder from the humiliation of opening that attachment. How it alerted our IT department and blasted from the speakers on my computer at my cubicle. How my brother's normally cool face was screwed up and red with horror. Sure, he knew I wasn't capable of being some sicko but with his own job on the line, he fired me.

That shit stings.

The only reason I didn't have the police knocking at my door was because the IT department finally ascertained it was the only dirty thing on my computer after a careful scrub down of my hard drive. They stood by their reason to end my employment, but they never involved the police.

I spend many sleepless nights wondering if Chelsea

sent it to me on purpose. For four months, I've obsessed over it. Now, I'm over it. I'm tired of letting Tucker Advertising control my life. They lost that control the moment my brother handed me the box to pack my shit.

A buzz comes from my phone, and I smile wondering if it's Buttercup. When I swipe the screen, I grin.

Buttercup: He truly is a horrible human being but he didn't deserve those insults. And you didn't deserve them by accident. Again, forgive me.

For a guy who hasn't smiled in a while, I've done a lot of that in the past six hours or so. All from a stranger's texts that weren't even for me.

Me: I'll forgive you if you tell me your name, Buttercup.

The three dots on my screen move as she replies.

Buttercup: I don't give my name out to strangers.

I snort.

Me: But you give them verbal lashings instead? You at least owe me your name…

It only takes her a moment to respond.

Buttercup: Tell me yours first, please.

Please? I smirk. She sounds cute. I shake my head because for all I know "she" could be a "he."

Me: Ram.

This time, her response is immediate.

Buttercup: Like a goat? With horns?
Me: Like I haven't heard that one before. Baaaaaad joke, Buttercup.

While I await her response, I open up Photoshop and

begin working on the logo for Inigo. I'm so sucked into my design that I miss her next couple of responses.

Buttercup: Why do you call me Buttercup?

Buttercup: I'm sorry if I offended you.

Buttercup: That's not really your name.

Buttercup: OMG. I've offended you twice in the past nine hours.

I jolt up and check the clock. I'm supposed to meet Roman in an hour. I haven't showered or anything. But the logo looks badass. I've found my groove again, thank fuck.

Me: You accused me of killing your father. Would you prefer I call you Inigo? I mean... I still haven't established if you're a chick or a dude.

Buttercup: Ahhh. *The Princess Bride*. I'm surprised you caught that.

I grin as I respond.

Me: At least I know we're from the same generation. At least I hope you are.

Me: Tell me you're at least 18.

The very thought of texting with a teenager after my kiddie porn mishap makes me shudder.

Buttercup: 25. Tell me you're at least under forty.

I laugh as I type.

Me: 30. Was your dickhead ex an old geezer? Also...you never told me your sex.

Quickly, I hop in the shower. I don't have time to shave off my scruff, but I'm kind of liking it now. After working at Tucker Advertising and dealing with their shitty dress code for three years, I'm enjoying the non-robot look. I brush my teeth in warp speed and style my hair in a messy way before throwing on a pair of holey jeans and a white Clash T-shirt. I frown when I realize it's gotten smaller.

And no, I haven't turned into a fat ass.

Opposite actually.

When you can't sleep at night, sometimes lifting weights is the only thing to keep a person sane. I'll need to buy some new shit if I continue to get more built. I grab my leather jacket and stuff my feet into my combat boots before heading out the door. While I walk to the parking lot where my old Mustang is, I check to see if Buttercup has responded.

>**Buttercup:** I'm a girl.
>**Buttercup:** I mean…a woman. Gah!
>**Buttercup:** I'm not good with people. Clearly.
>**Buttercup:** Sorry, Mr. Stranger. Er, Ram. I've already creeped on this little conversation too much. Hope you have a nice life.

I stop just as I get to my car that my dad and I rebuilt before he passed away ten years ago.

>**Me:** Glad to know you're a woman. And newly single from my observation. You don't get off that easy…unless you want to. ;) What's your name?

The three dots are immediate, like she was waiting for my text. The thought warms me.

>**Buttercup:** Carrie.
>**Me:** Like Stephen King's? The one covered in pig's blood?
>**Buttercup:** No! Like Underwood!!

Me: Hmmm. Can't say I've ever heard of her. Perhaps you should send me a picture of yourself.

I climb into the car and turn over the engine. The loud rumble is my favorite part of this car. Every time I get in, though, I think of Dad. My chest aches a bit, and I absently rub my fist over it.

Buttercup: Fat chance, mister! How do I know you aren't some creepy stalker who is going to do nasty things with my picture?

I laugh out loud before firing off my response.

Me: Define nasty.

Feeling brave, I take a selfie but crop off my head.

Me: If it makes you feel any better, you can do nasty things with my picture. Again...define nasty.

I don't wait for a response because I'll be late to meet Roman if I don't leave now. The entire drive, I can't help but feel excitement bubbling just below the surface. I hadn't realized just how depressed I was until the fog seemed to lift a bit. I'm not sure if I've even left the house in weeks. Roman's concern had become permanently etched in his furrowed brow. And Mom called more than I could handle. Hell, he even roped in our little sister, Reagan, who's in college in California. They were coming at me on all fronts.

The person to pull me out of the haze, though, was an absolute stranger with her random quote from *The Princess Bride*.

When I pull up in front of the tavern and park in one

of the open spaces, I look back at my phone.

Buttercup: You're a baaaad billy goat.

Buttercup: OMG...I offended you again.

Buttercup: I was just teasing.

Buttercup: I'm so sorry.

I shake my head and fire off another text.

Me: I'm not the old cheating geezer. It takes a lot more than a cheesy joke to hurt my feelings. What does wound me is the fact you feel you need to apologize for everything. You don't know me and yet you're worried about upsetting me. Who are you, Buttercup?

Three dots moving.

Buttercup: I'm a mess. And I actually just apologized again. You should be proud though because I deleted it. I'm not sorry! There!

I grin because I can almost imagine her triumphant smile.

Buttercup: Is that really your picture or are you catfishing me?

Snorting, I reply.

Me: It's me. And now I'm sitting in a parking spot waiting to meet someone for lunch yet here I am texting with you. Even though I don't know who you are.

She responds almost immediately.

Buttercup: I don't do cheaters. Does she know you're texting with a stranger? Does she know you're wanting to do nasty

things with my picture? Huh, asshole, huh?

I get out of my car and stride over to the front door where my brother is waiting. Before he can argue, I snap another selfie. This time of the two of us. Again, I crop out our heads.

Me: Well, she's a he so there's that. And he's my brother. So there's that too.

My brother gives me a quizzical look before holding the door open for me. We pile into our favorite booth inside while I wait for her to reply.

Buttercup: OMG. I'm so sorry.

Buttercup: Dang!!

Buttercup: Well at least you know why he cheated on me. :(

At her last text, anger surges through me.

Me: He cheated because he's a dick.

Roman's brows are lifted as he watches me text my new friend. When she replies, I return my attention to my phone.

Buttercup: I need to get back to work. Can we pick back up on this later? You know… so I can formally apologize for being rude. Again.

I scratch at the stubble on my jaw and smile.

Me: As you wish.

Chapter Three

Dani

> ## Oops, I did it Again

"PLEASE STOP LAUGHING." THAT'S ME WITH MY hands covering my face, while Andie is practically rolling on the floor laughing at my embarrassing expense.

"Girl, I can't. It's just that… That…" She buckles over again in a fit of giggles. "And… and… Carrie? Really?"

I know I said I wouldn't hurt a fly, but I'm about to tackle my best friend to the ground. "I panicked. I didn't want to give him my real name. What if he's like some psychopath?"

She snorts. "I doubt that. If he was able to replay lines from *The Princess Bride*, I'm guessing he's more like some nerd who sits at home reading his comic books."

"Well, what's wrong with that? That means he has a hobby," I argue.

Andie rolls her eyes, mouthing *ew*, while she counts her drawer. She has been having a great laugh at my expense ever since I walked into the bank for work. I can't say I have ever been so drunk in my life. Ashamed that I could barely remember how I got home or who undressed me, which was no one since I woke up in my clothes from the previous night. I also woke up to a long text message thread with a complete stranger. *I can suck great dick? Really Danielle?*

Mortified was putting it lightly on how I felt as I read through them. Those crude messages were *not* me. I barely swear. I *never* swear, but in one night, I decided to start drinking and go all out, bringing out this person I never knew existed. I was so embarrassed that after an hour of pacing my small apartment, I texted the stranger back, telling him I was sorry. Surprisingly, he texted me right back. And with each message, I found myself less embarrassed and more intrigued about who he was. He had just received some pretty insane messages from a stranger, but here he was texting back like we were old friends, bantering over a secret joke. And the fact that he got my *The Princess Bride* comment made me strangely elated. Being that it was one of my favorite movies. Daryl probably couldn't even tell me my middle name. Let alone could he be bothered to care about my interests. But in this complete stranger, I found something in common.

Throughout the morning, while getting ready for work, we messaged back and forth. His replies all made me smile and as I tried to match his humor, I kept falling short. Each time I tried to make a funny, the messages would stop and I would panic, pacing my room while smacking my head, telling myself I did it again. I was making a complete fool out of myself.

But when he had to go asking for names, I freaked. I said my name was Carrie. Why? I have *no* idea. It could have been that Carrie Underwood was playing softly on the television while I made my breakfast, but I'm not sure why it wasn't my real name that came out. Maybe because I was enjoying the banter with this complete stranger and it felt a bit liberating to talk to someone who wasn't already judging me. He had no idea that I was just a mousy little thing, no backbone, no great story, and definitely no modeling gigs lined up. I was simple. Boring. Andie called me the cutest little pushover she'd ever met.

There is just something to be said about getting to talk freely to a complete stranger without having to out your real self, and I was kind of enjoying my new friend. *Ram.* Strange name. At first I thought he was lying to me. Maybe that's why I spit out Carrie instead of Danielle, or Dani as my close friends call me.

Okay, so I'm a super shy loner with one close friend. Andie. Well, her full name is Andrea. When we were kids, a group of mean girls used to pick on me. I have always been small and mousy. My boobs didn't come in until way past the acceptable age for horny teenage boys and I just didn't have that high school luster like most girls had. I also dressed like a boy. Thanks to my mom and her church-going ways. The girls would always tease me, calling me Dani Boy, poking fun. I, of course, did nothing because I was shy. But Andrea stuck up for me, swapping out one girl's shampoo for glue in gym class and snuck chocolate laxatives in another's purse during lunch. But what she did that told me she was truly my friend was that she shortened her name to Andie, so she too would have a boy's name. She told me I had to overcome them. To be better than them. Embrace the name. And "*Fuck 'em*." Her words. So we did.

We've been at work for only an hour and I'm itching to check my phone. I wonder if he is done with his lunch. If he's texted me back. I don't know why he would. I'm just technically a wrong number to him. But that picture. I wish he would've included his face. The curiosity of what he looks like eats at me while I help each customer who walks into the bank.

"Hey, Dani." I turn to see Frank, another bank teller, standing next to me with *that* look. An expectant one. One that tells me he's about to ask a favor.

"Hey, Frank," I answer in a curt tone. "How are you today? How's Milly?"

"Oh, she's fine. Thanks again for taking her to the vet for me. Really helped." I sure hope it did, since I also ended up picking up his vet bill and am still waiting for him to pay me back. "So, I have a big favor. I have a date tonight, and I really need to get off early. You would be a life saver if you could pick up my last two hours tonight." Two hours? I've been here all day and I picked up his late shift last week as well. I was hoping to go home and organize my finances since I need to figure out how I'm going to replenish my bank account. I want to say no, but I don't know how. I would feel bad if he couldn't go on his date.

"Sur—"

Before I can finish, I yelp because someone kicks me in the side of my ankle. I turn to see Andie giving me the crazy eye.

"What did you do *that* for?" I hiss, rubbing my ankle where I know she's just left a bruise.

"Backbone, girl!"

I shake my head at her, and then turn back to Frank. "That would be fin—"

Again, she kicks me.

I turn and grumble. "Stop! Please."

Back to Frank, I start, "I—"

"She would *not* like to pick up your extra hours, Frank," Andie interrupts. "And I'm sure your Tinder date will wait until you get off work. Trust me. The darker it is out for her, the better."

My jaw drops at her rude comment. Frank doesn't say anything more. He gives Andie a nasty look and walks back to where he came from.

"Why did you do that?" I huff, still nursing my ankle. "That was extremely rude."

"Um, because it was *extremely* rude of him to take advantage of you like that. He does it every week. And he knows you'll say yes. He's a total douche and doesn't deserve your kindness. Half of America doesn't deserve it. That's why you need to stop handing it out like it's free."

But isn't kindness kinda free?

"Dani, stop," she says softly at the confused look I'm giving her. "You know what I mean. You need to stop letting people walk all over you. Say no to people. Say yes when it's deserved." She shuts her drawer and comes into my teller space. "Listen. We are on a mission to toughen you up."

I look at her quizzically. I'm not sure there's hope to

get me muscles, I weigh a whopping one hundred and twenty-five, sopping wet. "I really don't want to work out, Andie," I tell her.

A big sigh leaves her lips as she brings her hands to my shoulders. "Dani, listen. You are too nice. And one day, it's going to take a toll. You'll have had enough and snap. And not in a good way. I'm talking like Brittany Spears, 2006, snap. And I will be the first person to tell you, you will *not* look good bald. You need to grow a backbone."

"How does one grow a backbone? I thought we were born with them?"

Andie starts shaking me. "Earth to Dani! It's just an expression. You need to say no to people! Like Frank and all his stupid favors. Like Janice who sweet-talked you into trading sandwiches with her at lunch last week. Like the customer who convinced you to keep your register open after closing because *he* was late. Just Say No!"

"But I'm not—"

"No."

"Yeah, but—"

"No!"

"I get it bu—"

"JUST SAY NO! I swear, you're like a walking anti-drug commercial."

Darn it. I *am* like a *just-say-no* ad. I straighten my shoulders and arch my back. Taking in a deep breath, I say, "Fine. Try me. Ask me something."

Her eyes light up. "Hey Dani, can you take my whole week's worth of shifts? My vagina flared up again and I need to soak it in Vagisil."

A smile breaches my lips. But I keep a straight face.

"No, Andie. I will not."

She nods in approval. "Good job. Okay, but will you come over and cook me dinner? Then do my laundry? Then pay my cable bill?"

"No, I will not." I repeat, feeling empowered by this new word. Andie smiles, patting me on the back. "Good work!" She turns to close out her register. "But hey, do you mind counting my drawer so I can ditch out of here early?"

"Sure—"

"NO!"

I jump, along with a few customers, and Bill, the customer service manager, as her answer echoes throughout the bank.

"The answer is no, Dani! No, no, no!"

Darn it! She tricked me! A total setup!

"No matter who asks," she tells me firmly. "Even me. The answer is no."

Andie spent the rest of our workday throwing questions at me, and I was on alert with every question. I said no to every single one, even the one where she asked me who kept texting me.

"No, you can actually answer this one. Who's texting you? Your phone keeps lighting up."

I fumble for my phone, nearly dropping it in the process, as I yank it up from the counter. I look at my screen to see not one, but three text messages from Ram.

Ram: I had a hot dog for lunch. Thought about you and that mouth you talked up.

Ram: Okay I was joking. That was kind of a dick thing to say.

Ram: No pun in the dick comment either. Shit, sorry. Look, now I'm the one apologizing.

I laugh at his last message.

"What's so funny? Let me see!" Andie grabs for my phone, but I pull back. She gives me her crazy look and puts her hands on her hips. "Show me or I'll start telling everyone you're messing around with Frank." My lips purse at the gross thought of doing *anything* with Frank. She sees it and smiles, knowing she won. I show her my phone and she reads my latest text.

"Damn. Potty mouth. He's still texting you?"

"Yeah, I guess." I blush, feeling embarrassed at the excitement this complete stranger creates in me.

"Well, hell, I mean I would probably keep texting you too, if you admitted you had great tits and suck a mean nob." I smack her in the shoulder as she busts out laughing. As she's still holding my phone, another text comes through.

"Oh my, you have a Chatty Kathy on your hands," she says as she hands my phone back.

Ram: Okay, now I feel like a jerk. I really didn't mean it like that. I'm not like that. Rude, I mean. I'm actually a really nice guy. Now I'm babbling and you may have already blocked this number. I'll stop now. Nice knowing you, Buttercup.

I read the message and grin.

"Ew, are you smiling at your phone?"

I raise my head. "What?"

"You. You're smiling. Like someone just complimented your troll collection. Do you like *like* this guy or something?"

"No! I don't even know him." He's just… just…

"Whatever, liar. You're giving your phone the googly eyes. Dude, no way. This is called rebound… Or wait… maybe we can…" I can see the wheels turning. "Okay. Respond back to him. He is going to be our guinea pig."

Guinea pig? "And how exactly is he going to be our guinea pig?"

"Simple. You're going to boss him around. Be blunt. Practice your backbone." She must see that I'm not following, because she snatches my phone and starts typing off a reply message.

Me: Prove it.

"Prove it? What's that supposed to mean?"

"Well, he said he's not usually rude. Have him prove it. We want him growling in hunger for you, got it?" I highly doubt anyone is growling over me. The ding comes back through and we both throw our eyes to my phone.

Ram: I tipped the waitress extra today because she told me her son needed money for his book fair.

I *awww* at his message while Andie does a huge *pfft*, then she starts jamming on my phone.

Me: Sounds like something any normal Joe would do. Does that mean you wouldn't normally donate money to a cause? Are you some sort of money hogger?"

"What is *that* supposed to mean?" I gape at her

message.

"It'll allow us to figure out what he does. Make sure he's not a loser like Daryl."

Another message flows through.

Ram: I am a successful businessman, yes, and I donate money all the time. I actually gave her a $100 tip. It was important to me that her son gets those books.

"You just did it again."

I look up, my cheeks heating. "Did what?"

"Googly eyed your phone."

Ugh, oops, I totally just did it again.

Chapter Four

Ram

> ### Define Nasty

'M AN ASSHOLE.

I stare down at my phone and groan. Did I really just brag about something I didn't do to a person I don't know? I've sunk to a new low. Lying.

Scrubbing my palm up and down over my scruffy cheek, I let out a sigh. I'm flat broke until Inigo Photog signs a contract with me. So it was my brother who bought lunch. It was Roman who flirted with the waitress. It was Roman who left an over-the-top tip because he also left his card. He wasn't paying for some kid's books. My brother was attempting to get the pretty blonde waitress in the sack.

I settle in my desk chair and fire off an email to Victor Masters, Inigo's owner, after attaching some of my design concepts for the logo and branding along with the mockup for the website. Roman, over lunch, suggested I hit up some of Tucker Advertising's old clients who no longer use them. The ones I had a good relationship with in the past. While I wait for Carrie to respond to my stupid text, I message a few potential clients.

Eventually, she responds.

> **Buttercup: Sorry, I got a customer and then another. We got slammed. Sounds like you're a generous guy. So what exactly is it you do anyway? You mentioned you were a businessman.**

Grumbling, I let my fingers hover over the screen. Do I lie again? Will she keep talking to me if she knows I'm technically unemployed?

She's just a stranger.

And even though I keep telling myself that, the guilt remains.

> **Me: I'm a marketing manager over the account execs at an ad firm. What do you do?**

Fuck.

I've once again told her I was my brother.

> **Buttercup: I'm a bartender.**

I wish I knew what she looked like so I could imagine her slinging drinks around at the bar. Would she wear cute little black shorts that showed off her toned legs? Would she lean over the bar counter to pass the drinks and show off her cleavage?

My cock decides it likes this fantasy of Buttercup the Bartender. I haven't been laid since the night before I got fired. Chelsea came over and I now realize that was a goodbye fuck. There was no cuddling after. She even made sure to grab a few things she'd left in my room, claiming she needed to get them dry cleaned.

Me: Which bar? I'd love to come see you one day?

Her response is quick.

Buttercup: I don't know you so I better not tell.

I roll my eyes.

Me: We could know each other. In fact….

I go into my contacts and dial her number. I'm not sure why I didn't consider calling her until this moment. It rings and rings, but she doesn't pick up. Maybe her voicemail will confirm that her name is Carrie too. I'm mildly annoyed she isn't answering because I know her phone is in her hand. Eventually, a soft, sultry voice recording plays in my ear.

"Hey," she says, pausing as if to consider what to say next. "It's me. You know what to do. Umm…" Another pause. "Just leave a message after the beep. Wait. Do cell phones even beep?" A woman laughs in the background causing Carrie to growl. It's an adorable sound…like a kitten trying to sound like a mountain lion. "Just leave your message. Bye."

It's by far the cutest voicemail greeting I've ever heard. My smile is immediate.

"I'm not sure why you're avoiding picking up but at least I've confirmed you're a chick," I say with a chuckle. "I've also confirmed you have a nice voice. Would it make me a creepy stalker if I called again just to hear it?" I grunt. "Yeahhhhh, so it would. Anyway, I just wanted to say hi. Like actually *say* it. So you could know I'm normal too. Although, there's nothing probably normal about this phone call." I pause and roll my eyes at myself. I'm a fucking idiot. She'll probably take one listen and move on. The mystery was better. I should have just kept letting her think I was a badass. "I'm glad you texted me by mistake," I utter. "It's been the most fun I've had in four months." Another pause as I clench my eyes closed. "I'm sorry I called. This was out of line. But I'm not sorry I got to hear your voice. Enjoy your day, Buttercup."

I hang up and abandon my phone. With a huff of frustration, I peel away my shirt and go on a hunt for some gym shorts. I'll lift some weights to clear my head. Calling her unexpectedly was a dick move. If I were her, I'd block my number and move the fuck on. Once I've dressed in a pair of shorts and thrown on some tennis shoes, I bypass a shirt and stand in front of my long bedroom mirror.

Roman and I are similar in the looks department, down to our size and height. We even share the same pale brown eyes that our sister, Reagan, is jealous of. It's our mannerisms that are different. Roman is more scowly. Typically, I'm more smiley. He keeps his hair shorter and styled in a neat, professional way. Mine is longer and unruly, styled more in a just-fucked kind of way. The biggest difference is our chests. My brother is a weirdo about tattoos. Mom's warning somehow sticks in his head.

Get a tattoo and I'll disown you.

I smirk thinking about the time when I turned eighteen and I showed my mom my first tattoo. That woman beat me upside the head with the romance novel she was reading. But she didn't disown me. And I continued to get them until my solid chest was nothing but a canvas of colorful art. I'd been dying to get a sleeve next, but my brother lectured me for a week about how unprofessional that was. I'm still undecided. The longer I remain unemployed, the more tempted I am to say "fuck professionalism" and do what I want.

Flexing my chest, I wonder if Carrie would be impressed by my tats. I'm almost considering taking a selfie of them to show her, but wisely steer myself out of my bedroom toward the room we use as a gym. Sending her an unrequested naked chest picture is almost as bad as an unwanted dick pic.

I've definitely reached an all-time low. I need to lift and clear my head.

This stranger is scrambling my brain.

After a shower, I make my way back to my room in nothing but a towel. I'm dreading reading her response to my phone call. I missed many and I can only imagine what they'll say. Biting the bullet, I snatch up my phone and lie down on my bed. My towel pulls open and my dick flops out. I need to just go out with Roman and pick up some chick for the night. Because I'm long overdue for some pussy and my mind has seemed to latch on to this stranger.

I close my eyes and think about her voice.

So sweet and soft.

Apologetic.

Just hearing how nice she seemed pisses me off. Her

ex sounds like an asshole to let someone like her go. Hell, I've barely been talking to her for two days and I can already tell she's interesting, quirky, and cute. And I'm dying to know her better.

I pop my eyes open and force myself to read her response.

>**Buttercup:** You called me!
>**Buttercup:** OMG.
>**Buttercup:** I like your voice too.
>**Buttercup:** You don't have to feel bad about calling me. I just couldn't take your call at work.
>**Buttercup:** Are you hiding from me now?
>**Buttercup:** COME BACK!
>**Buttercup:** OMG that sounded so desperate. I was being playful. OMG texting doesn't show jokes very well. Crap!
>**Buttercup:** I'm serious though. Why'd you leave? Your voice sounds a;sldjfa;ksf
>**Buttercup:** FUCKIN' HOT! I'D RIDE THAT MOUTH ALL THE WAY INTO TOMORROW!

I snort at that response.

>**Buttercup:** OMG!!!! That bitch stole my phone! I didn't type that! Kill me now.

And then no more texts. But I'm smiling rather than scowling now. My dick is also hard and in my hand. Jesus, what is this stranger doing to me?

>**Me:** Send me a picture so I know you're a woman. Please.

My fist goes up and down around my rigid cock. I

close my eyes, wondering what she looks like. While I can't figure her face out, I imagine her being kind of shy. A cute smile that she hides sometimes. Her cheeks turning pink when I whisper naughty things into her ear.

The phone buzzes and my eyes bug at the response.

Buttercup: <PHOTO ATTACHED>

I swipe it open to look at the picture. As soon as I see it, I start laughing so hard. She took a picture of her hand. A thumbs up. It's so fucking corny, but I can't stop chuckling. I scan the picture for clues and I can tell she's at the bank now. Zooming in, I smile when I see the bank name on a pen.

We bank at the same place. Small world. At least I know she lives in town.

Me: That's a sexy thumbs up. You don't want to see my thumbs up right now.

I smirk knowing my thumb is around my aching cock.

Buttercup: Show me.

My eyes close as I fist myself harder. I'd love nothing more than to show her what I'm doing. All it would take was one picture. But I'm not a freak. Well, she doesn't know that at least.

I reopen my eyes and respond.

Me: My hand is a little busy. ;)

While I wait for her to respond, I stroke my cock as I stare at her delicate hand. A dainty bracelet hangs from her thin wrist and her thumbnail is painted navy blue. One side has chipped off. Her hand would barely wrap around my dick, and that thought has me grunting out my release all over my belly.

Buttercup: You ARE doing nasty things

with my picture.

I grin as I clean myself up with my towel.

Me: Define nasty…

Buttercup: Did you…OMG how do I say this without sounding stupid? Whack off?

Snorting, I sit up and locate a pair of sweatpants. I slide them on without underwear and lie back down on the bed.

Me: Men aren't as strong as women. They see something beautiful that turns them on and they take action.

The three dots on her end move as she types.

Buttercup: You're so bold, Ram. I would never do something like that.

I frown and run my fingers through my wet hair.

Me: You're hiding behind a screen. I don't know you. You don't know me. It's easy to feel brave that way. Maybe next time you'll send me more than your hand…

She responds immediately.

Buttercup: Maybe next time you'll send more than your T-shirt.

At this, I laugh.

Me: So someone IS a lot braver behind text. And fine. Don't say I never gave you anything.

I take a selfie of my chest, making sure to crop out my face again. When I look at the picture, you can see part of my mouth that's quirked up into a half smirk. I decide I'll give her that too. I hit send before I change my mind.

She doesn't respond, and I'm distracted when my

brother knocks on my door. I didn't realize it was after five already.

"Come in," I holler.

He pushes through the door wearing a tired expression. Tucker Advertising has been sucking the life out of him for so long. I wish he'd just leave that fucking place already. When I'd gotten canned, I'd half expected him to follow not far behind. He didn't, and I'm a little frustrated that he chose his career over his own blood.

"Let's go out tonight. We'll go bar hopping. I've had a rough day and need to get laid," he grunts out as he loosens his tie. His eyes roam over me and then flit to my desk. "Did Inigo respond?"

I shrug my shoulders and rest my phone on my toned stomach. "Not yet. I did like you said, though, and messaged several old Tucker clients. I'm hoping someone will bite."

He nods his approval. "Good work. Did your business cards come in? You should be spending your days out doing cold calls."

"Okay, Dad."

We both wince at my response, but my brother changes the subject quickly.

"Old man Tucker is thinking of selling. At least that's what I heard through the grapevine. I don't like the idea of my job being in limbo," he utters and gives me a solemn stare. "I need this job."

I roll out of bed and saunter over to the closet in search of something to wear. Given that Roman is still wearing his suit means we'll hit up some of the fancier bars he likes to go to. I rummage around in my closet until I find a button-up shirt that doesn't need ironing. It's black and looks nice enough. I'm not wearing a tie, nor am I wearing slacks. This is the best he'll get from me. "Why do you need that job so bad? You're good at what you do. Any ad firm would be lucky to have you."

As I dress, he sits at my desk and messes around on my computer with his back to me.

"I've been planning to leave for months now," he says, his voice low. The sting at him choosing them over me doesn't hurt so much knowing he's been thinking about it. "I just wanted to have all my ducks in a row before I leapt into something..." he trails off and clicks through the designs I've been working on. "Something more enjoyable. These are good designs, by the way. You haven't lost your touch."

"Thanks." I button up my shirt on the way to the bathroom. It takes a few minutes to style my hair in the just-fucked way that will hopefully get me laid. Although, I'd rather just have Carrie. I'm fucking attracted to her hand for crying out loud.

When I come back out, Roman is standing, a pensive look making his brows furrow together. I smirk because when Roman thinks with that look on his face, he gets shit done. I'm just wondering what world he's going to conquer next.

"You ready?"

I can't help but smile. Maybe if we hit enough bars, I'll eventually find the one Carrie works at.

"Ready as I'll ever be."

It's been three hours and she still hasn't responded. I know my chest looked good in that picture so she can't think I'm gross. That much I know for sure. So I wonder what has her ignoring my last text. I'm nursing my Jack and Coke, but Roman's knocking them back like the supply will be gone tomorrow and tonight's his last chance to have them. With each drink, he gets more playful and grabby with the servers. It's times like these he reminds me of the brother I had in high school. Before Dad passed away. I can't help but smile.

"I haven't seen you fellas around here before," a sultry voice coos from beside me. Pointy fingernails dig into my flesh through my shirt.

I turn to regard the woman who literally has her claws in me. Older. Maybe forty-ish. Fine lines and wrinkles carefully hidden behind a pound of makeup. Bright blue eyes that have seen better days. A painted red smile on her face. She seems like a lovely woman, but not my type. When I glance down at her red-painted fingernails that match her lips, I can't help but think of Carrie's navy blue thumbnail. It wasn't a long nail and had been clipped short.

"We don't make it out this way often," I agree with a forced smile.

She takes the smile as an invitation and sidles up on the stool beside me. "You should. A handsome guy like yourself should be spreading himself all over this town." She winks at me, and I suppress a shudder.

"Look…" I start but my phone buzzes in my pocket, distracting me.

Buttercup: Was that really you?

I grin and return her text.

Me: In the flesh.

Buttercup: Har de har har. I like the tribal arrowhead tattoo.

Me: I designed it myself actually.

Her response is immediate.

Buttercup: Wow! That's so cool! Behind the businessman is an artist?

I cringe at having almost outed myself on a lie. The woman beside me clears her throat to get my attention. When I turn to her, she's frowning.

"Look, honey," she says firmly. "If you're interested, my cost is a grand for the night."

I blink at her in confusion. "What?"

This time, she's the one confused. "I thought you wanted sex."

Boy, do I ever.

Just not with her.

"Not exactly—" I start, but my drunk brother interrupts by slapping a wad full of hundreds on the bar.

"My treat, bro," he says, smirking at me. His drink sloshes, and I realize he's fucking plastered.

Growling, I yank the money up and shove it into my pocket for safekeeping.

"Time to go, drunk ass," I grumble.

The other lady who had been making out with him a little bit ago protests at my pulling him away. I slap some cash onto the bar for our tab and drag my stumbling brother away from those old whores.

"Did you really bring us here so you could pay for sex?" I snap.

He mutters something about me needing sex to help with my creativity. His heavy arm is slung over my shoulder and I all but have to carry him from the bar. As soon as we push through the doors, I lose my grip on him and he crashes into a pair of women, knocking one to the pavement.

"DRUNK ASSHOLE!" The blonde shrieks, hauling off and kicking my brother who's all but tackled a brunette.

I grunt and pull him from the petite woman. I'm awarded a flash of her white panties as she tries to right her skirt. Watery hazel eyes meet mine as I pull my beast of a brother away from her. The blonde kicks him again, this time on his ass, which makes him bellow in faux pain. I need to get him home. But my eyes are locked on those of the brunette. Her pink lip is jutted out, and if I didn't have this stupid drunk oaf in my grip, I'd ask her if I could have a nibble of it.

The spell is broken when the blonde once again kicks my brother before helping the brunette to her feet.

"Oh my God," she shrieks, her hands smoothing out over the other woman's now messy hair, before handing her back her phone that had been sitting on the pavement. "Dani, are you okay?"

The brunette. Dani. She nods, her gaze never leaving mine as the blonde hauls her away from my blubbering brother.

"That blonde kicked my ass," he complains, waving his middle finger at her.

I mouth that I'm sorry to the frazzled brunette before turning and half carrying my dumb brother to my car.

"She literally fuckin' kicked my ass, man," he bellows. "I'm gonna have bruises and shit."

My normally composed brother curses like a sailor when he's tanked. I smirk and ruffle his now imperfect hair. "You deserved it, bro."

As soon as I load my brother into the passenger seat and buckle him up, I lean against the side of my car and check for any missed texts from Carrie.

Buttercup: I wish I was creativaslfa;lsdkfjsldkjfa

I frown, wondering if her friend stole her phone again. But this time, I don't receive any suggestive texts. Finally, another one comes through.

Buttercup: OMG what a night. I SO need a drink.

Smirking, I fire off a text.

Me: Well you do work in a bar so that should be easy. Cheers!

The next picture she sends is her same hand I received earlier with the same flecked navy blue polish. Except this time, she's not giving me a thumbs up. This time she's holding a glass of red wine.

I close my eyes and imagine the brunette from earlier. Her plump lips pressing against the edge of the glass. I've given my stranger fantasy the face of another. Until Carrie sends me a real picture, I won't feel guilty putting the pretty brunette there as a placeholder.

Me: What I wouldn't give to be there with you right now...

After sending that text, I climb into the 'Stang and fire up the engine. It's going to be hell getting my passed out brother up to the eighth floor of our building. But at least once I finally retire back to my bedroom, I can message Carrie without interruption.

Chapter Five

Dani

Junk in the Trunk

"**F**UCKING DRUNK ASSHOLES," ANDIE MUTTERS while walking into Bender's.

I look behind me at the glass door, trying to get a glimpse of the two guys we just ran into. Or more like one drunk guy plowed into me while his friend tried hoisting him back up. I strain my neck hoping to catch one last look. The way that guy looked at me. It felt strange. A complete stranger and the way he took me in, caught my breath. I couldn't even tell him I was all right, forcing myself to nod.

"Dude, what are you looking at?"

I turn back. "Nothing. Just those guys."

"Yeah, total assholes. Learn to handle your liquor, douchebags."

I lift my hand to defend the stranger. "I don't think the

other guy was drunk—"

"Who cares! Ew, I hate guys like that." We walk in, spotting Brett behind the bar, who seems to be enjoying a few laughs with Sylvia, Bender's longest lasting waitress.

"What's so funny?" Andie asks, sitting on the stool in front of Brett, myself next to her.

"Oh, look who the cat dragged in." Brett smiles, dropping two coasters in front of us. "Sylvia over here just had some fun, messing with some random. Told the guy she would give him the night of his life for a thousand bucks."

Sylvia starts laughing again. "You should have seen his face. Pale as a ghost." She slaps her thigh, letting out a loud chuckle.

"So what can I get you two ladies tonight? Another tequila bender?"

I cringe at that word. I really, if possible, never want to hear *that* word ever again. "I would like a glass of wine, please," I kindly ask. Andie orders a vodka tonic. Brett tends to the bar and, shortly after, is placing a glass of merlot in front of me, a vodka tonic in front of Andie.

"How's the breakup going?" Brett asks while I snap a pic of my wine.

Shrugging Brett off, I open my text messages and see the last message from *him*. The photo of his chest. The second I saw it, I threw my phone, almost embarrassed that I saw his bare chest. All those tattoos. His defined abs. I was getting heated in the cheeks just thinking about it. I definitely didn't expect him to be so… so colorful. But it worked on him. I imagined myself taking my nails and softly scratching down that chest, my curiosity at what was below building. My cheeks turn crimson at the indecent thoughts. I turn to Andie, who is downing her drink. Turning back to my phone, I start to message when Andie startles me, attempting to snatch it from my hand.

"Seriously! Give me that."

"No!" I say as we wrestle for my phone. I finally win and she gives up.

"Well, *Brett*," Andie answers for me, "the breakup is going great. No peep about the cheating fuckhead. And *that's* because she is all over Wrong Number's balls!"

At that I look up from my text. "I am not!"

"Then who did you just text? Certainly not your mom."

I give her my stink-eye, because I can't lie. But I *want* to talk to him. I regret not answering his call, but I panicked. When I saw his name come across my screen, I about tossed my phone at a customer's head like it was on fire. *He tried calling me.* I was in shock, and confused, then excited and even more curious as to why. But when I saw the notification that I had a voicemail, I had never requested a break so fast in my life. And it may have been the first time in all eternity that I just walked off before even hearing my boss's response.

And that voice. It was perfect. Deep, masculine. His laugh sending a warm sensation down below. I'd listened to it three times before my boss came back and told me my break was over. I knew it wasn't, but I also knew it was a busy time of day, so I nodded and went back to work.

Everything about him weighed heavy on my mind all day. And if it was true what he said, that he masturbated to my messages! A small laugh slips from my lips remembering his words—

"Hello! Earth to Dani!" I snap out of it, turning to Andie, who's staring me down, then to Brett and Sylvia, who both seem to be watching me expectantly.

"What? What did I miss?"

"Well, for starters the whole conversation," Andie snaps.

"Darlin', I just asked you why you're staring at your phone like someone just sent you a pic of a juicy steak?"

"Because she WANTS him to send a pic of his juicy steak!" Andie exclaims. "You should have seen the one he sent earlier. You would think she hadn't eaten in days the way she drooled over it."

I smack her in the arm. "I did not," I lie. Feeling guilty for lying, though, I try to explain. "Okay fine. I may have, but who wouldn't?! Even you said he was, your words, *super-hot, and fuckable*."

Andie shrugs her shoulders, agreeing, and takes a sip of her drink.

Brett raises an eyebrow looking at me curiously. "Wait, wrong number dude sent you a dick pic?"

"NO," I say, raising my voice, embarrassed. "No, he sent me a picture of his bare chest. A nice chest as a matter of fact." I take a hefty sip of my wine. This topic is becoming too uncomfortable for me. My phone dings and I look down to find a new message from Ram. I smile at his banter, flying off a response back, but when Brett sticks his hand out, I frown.

"Let me see it."

I look up just in time for Andie to grab my phone and hand it over to Brett. *Oh God.* I cover my eyes, but peek as I watch Brett scroll through the messages. His lips twitch as he reads. A few seconds pass and an eyebrow goes up. I groan into my hands as his manly chuckle fills the air. "Your guy get off on you?" He grins, waiting for an answer. I refuse to take my face out of my hands. "He's got some sweet ink, though. Buff dude."

I lift my face, knowing I have to face the music sooner or later. Brett is smiling at me, while Sylvia is now looking at my phone.

"I think they're pretty," I agree.

A loud chuckle startles me as Brett grabs his chest laughing. "Babe, don't ever tell a man his tattoos are *pretty*. That shit will never get you what you want."

"Well, what do you say then? I dig your zig-zags? And what exactly is it you think I want?"

Another laugh. "You mean his tribal art? Yeah, you say you dig it. You like it. Just leave off the word pretty." He hands me back my phone and I look closer at Ram's tattoos. I notice an arrowhead on his pectoral muscle. "Plus, you want the dick pic. Important to see what the dude's packin' before you commit."

This conversation cannot get any more embarrassing. I certainly don't want to see his *stuff*. I offer Brett a how-dare-he-assume look and turn to Andie, who is weirdly nodding.

"What? I do not!"

"Bull," she says with a chuckle. "And if you don't, I sure as hell do. That chest. Those tattoos. It *has* to come with a package any girl wants to bob on."

Ugh…

"So!" Andie claps her hands together, while I drain my whole glass of wine. "Tonight's mission is get a picture of Ram's cock."

UGH!

"Andie, no. I don't want—"

"We do," Sylvia and Andie reply in unison.

I groan. Then sigh. Then tap on my wine glass for a refill. "Fine."

It seems like everyone was already on board for the dick pic. Even Brett looked excited. I allow Andie to take the reins on this one because I can't say I know how to request a dick pic from a guy I barely know. Andie was more than delighted to take my phone and started typing off a quick message.

Me: I wish you would show me a dick pic.

"Andie, are you kidding me!? He's going to think I'm some sick weirdo!" I take my wine that Brett just refilled and chug a huge gulp. Before she even responds, we hear the ding, and all four of us lean in to see the phone. The message shows **<PHOTO ATTACHED>**.

"Oh my God, I can't look." I cover my eyes, but still peek a little.

"I can," Sylvia says, leaning over me to get a better gander. Andie opens it, and even though I'm too embarrassed to look, I sneak a glance through my fingers.

Ram: Like this?

And attached is a photo of a car taking up two parking spots.

"What the fuck!" Andie types away.

Me: No! What the fuck is this?

Ram: A dick. He took up two spaces. I had to park eons away from my loft.

I smile at his response. I am becoming a sucker for

his quirky humor.

Andie types another response.

Me: No, I mean your junk in your damn trunk.

We all stare at the phone as we see those three darn dots moving. Before we know it, another message with **<PHOTO ATTACHED>** comes through. This time, it's a picture of a car trunk.

Ram: I'm not really sure what's in it though. I broke the key in the lock ages ago.

I begin to laugh, along with Sylvia, who's also enjoying my guy, while Andie gets more annoyed.

"Seriously what's wrong with this dude? How does he not know what a dick is? He has one, right?" she grumbles.

"I'd assume he does since he jerked it off earlier," Brett says, putting his two cents in. That causes me to giggle, remembering our earlier text-versation.

Andie is next to me typing something like rapid fire.

Me: Let me put it in simple terms. Send me a picture of some cock.

"If he doesn't get that then you need to cut your losses like now with this dude."

We all stare at the phone and wait for Ram's reply. When we don't even get the three dots, I begin to worry we've offended him. I take another large gulp of my wine, worried that he got turned off by the aggressiveness of Andie's messages. I knew I shouldn't have let her do the texting.

Five more minutes, and then ten more pass and still no reply. My nerves are going berserk with the anxiety that

I just ruined what we were starting. I finish my second glass of wine, and then my third, when my phone finally dings. We all throw ourselves closer to the phone as Andie opens the newest **<PHOTO ATTACHED>**.

"Be a cock, be a cock," Andie chants out loud as she swipes and then, "Oh fucking come on!"

I can't hold in my laughter as we all look at a photo of a rooster.

Ram: You really are pushy. Fine here's a cock. Now you have to tell me what you plan on doing with it. Pet it? Rub it? I want every single dirty detail.

"This guy is ridiculous." Andie pouts, slamming her drink.

I smile at the photo. "I think he's charming."

She rolls her eyes at me, and I simply shrug. I think about how much I enjoy our text exchanges and how I want more. So much more. I climb off my stool, swaying a little from how fast I drank the three glasses of wine. I tell everyone that I have to go to the bathroom but find a quiet hallway.

I'm going to do it. I'm going to make a bold move and call him. I go to his contact info and my thumb hovers over the send button. "Don't be a scarcd-sally, Dani," I coach myself. I take in a deep breath, the feeling of the booze warming me from the inside out. It's giving me the liquid courage I need to just do it, and I do.

I press send.

And I hold my breath and close my eyes.

One ring. Two rings. On the third ring, I get his voice-mail. I let out the huge breath I was holding, feeling a bit disappointed. Why wouldn't he answer? Maybe he didn't want to talk to me.

"Ram. You know what to do." And the beep sounds in my ear.

"Um… Hi, it's me. I mean it's Da—Carrie. The one you've been texting. I mean, I think you probably know who I am. I, uh, I just wanted to tell you I liked your cock." I grin at his joke, but then realize how horrible that sounds. "Oh God! I didn't mean *your* cock. Oh crap, this is not going as I planned. I was hoping to talk, and we could get to know each other on a better level. I mean… not that I'm not enjoying us now. I like you. I mean! Oh my God! That sounds overboard since I don't even know you. Or you me. But I like our texts. Annnd, this was also maybe a bad idea." I huff in frustration. "Let's just pretend this never happened. Mmmkay? This is the wine calling. Don't worry about calling her back." I snort at my lame joke. Am I really this goofy? Apparently, I am. A huge groan comes from me. "Oh God!" And I hang up because I'm not sure I could fit any more awkwardness into one phone call.

Talk about first impressions.

Mine was impressionable, all right…

Chapter Six

Ram

> ## What Do We Have to Lose, Buttercup?

NE MISSED CALL.

Goddammit! I took a shower after my brother barfed all over us in the elevator and ended up missing her call. But the voicemail was worth it. Her voice was so unsure and she kept stumbling over her words. It was fucking adorable.

> **Me: Loved your message. I'm glad you liked my cock. Did you like my dick?**

Her response is immediate.

> **Buttercup: Are you this brave just because we're texting?**
>
> **Me: Why don't you call me again and find out?**

I have to wait a minute before she responds back.

> **Buttercup: I have an audience here at the**

bar. I'll call when I get back home. Deal?

Grinning, I type out a reply.

Me: I can't wait to hear your voice, Carrie.

She doesn't reply for what feels like hours. While I wait, I check on my passed out brother and straighten up the house. Then, when she still hasn't responded, I work on sending out more messages to potential clients. When it's nearly two in the morning, I get a call. The name Buttercup flashes on the screen. I've saved her thumbs up as her profile picture. I pick up on the second ring.

"Hello?"

It's quiet on her end. I can hear soft breathing.

"Carrie?"

A sigh into the phone. "I like when you call me Buttercup." There's a twinge of guilt in her tone.

"I like when you send me pictures of yourself, Buttercup," I say, indulging her. She giggles, and I swear to God, it's the sweetest sound ever. I turn off the lights in the house and lock up while I await her response. Eventually, she does.

"Umm," she breathes. "I'm not really good at this."

I chuckle. "What? Talking to people? You're a bartender. Isn't that part of the job requirement?"

Another soft sigh. Her sighs are cute. "What I mean is…I'm not normally a risk taker. I do everything traditionally and by the book. Texting with some random stranger. Talking about sex with him. Sending and receiving pictures with him. It's all so…"

"Risky?" I quip.

"Yeah."

I lie down on my bed in my darkened room and rest

a palm on my bare stomach. "Isn't risk all about the potential of losing something you once had? Like certain investments are risky because you chance losing money. What do we have to lose, Buttercup?"

She's silent for a moment. "I'm embarrassed."

"About having fun? About talking to someone who really wants to talk to you? Tell me why that embarrasses you."

"Well…" she trails off. A small, non-humorous laugh escapes her. "It's kind of weird. Like…ummm…gah."

"I like you, too." I scrub at my face in the darkness and let out a sigh of my own. "Look," I tell her. "I haven't exactly been happy for several months now. It wasn't until your wrong text that I began to laugh again. It may sound stupid, but I felt like you kind of dropped into my life at exactly the right moment."

She doesn't respond right away. Then, I hear her shuffling around. "What exactly are we doing? Are we trying to be friends?" Her words are breathy like she's doing stuff.

"We already are friends," I tell her, a smile curving my lips up. "We're trying to be more."

"I'm not sure I'm ready for that yet. I don't do relationships that often. Especially with people I don't know," she clips out.

I try not to sigh in frustration. "You keep saying you don't know me. Let's get to know each other. We'll make it fun."

"Okay." She's hesitant, but I'd do anything to keep her soft, breathy voice on the line.

"Tell me ten of your favorite things. Just real quick. I'll go first so you know what I mean. Ready?" I ask.

Silence and then, "Ready."

"Football. Photoshop. Mushroom pizza. Thunderstorms. Coffee. Muscle cars. *Game of Thrones.* Cats. Rollercoasters. And *The Princess Bride.* There, ten things. Your turn."

She giggles, and my cock twitches in response. My mind imagines the brunette from the bar earlier but with Carrie's voice. I know what I'll be thinking of later when my fist is gripping my dick.

"Okay, so um, let me think." She pauses for nearly a minute, clearly having to think hard about this. "Oh! I know! I love cats, too. I have a cat named Marilyn Manson—"

"Wait, what?" I interrupt, a chuckle vibrating my chest. "You named your cat after Marilyn Manson?"

She scoffs. "My cat, Manson for short, has white eyes and black fur. He's a little on the creepy side to outsiders, but I think he's quite handsome. Also, whenever I play Marilyn Manson, he sits in front of the iPod dock and stares. His tail flicks back and forth eagerly. He's done this ever since he was a bitty kitty, so it seemed fitting. Anyway," she huffs, "as I was saying. I also love saltwater taffy. Like, oh my God, it's the best ever. My parents used to take us to Silver Dollar City in Branson every Christmas and I was the proverbial kid in a candy shop. I'd sit there for hours watching them make the taffy. They had big machines they'd use to stretch it out. It was fascinating to watch. Then, once my parents got tired of that, they'd let me pick out a bagful of the stuff to take back home with us. All was well until I got my first cavity."

Chuckling, I absently run my fingers along the lines of

my abs. "I like that your ten things all have a story behind them. Go on. What's the third thing?"

"Um, three. My best friend, Andie. She's a godsend. We're joined at the hip and my life would be boring without her. Andie pushes me to be brave when I'm afraid. She encourages me when I feel down. She makes me dress like a ho sometimes when we go dancing because she says every woman has to go through their ho stage so they'll be ready to settle down when the time comes." She pauses and groans. "Oh my God. I just ramble, don't I? You just rattled your ten things off and I'm giving you TMI about each of mine. I'm sorry."

At this, I growl. "Don't ever apologize for being you. I happen to really like you. If I weren't talking to you right now, I'd be staring up at my ceiling in the dark, obsessing over my life. I'd replay my past in different ways, wondering how I could change things. I'd also worry over my future. And then, when the sun peeked through my windows in the morning, I'd shower and start my day, only to end it in the exact same way." This time, it's me who gives away too much information.

"When do you sleep?" she questions, her voice but a whisper.

"Honestly? Not much in the past few months. I've been dealing with some shit. I'll get past it. This insomnia crap became a way of life after my dad died ten years ago. It seems when I'm stressed, I can't sleep," I admit.

"I'm sorry about your dad," she murmurs. This time, I don't get on to her for apologizing. Because this time, I sense how genuine she is about the words. It makes my chest ache a little, so I change the subject.

"Tell me more of your favorite things."

I can hear a smile in her voice. "Okay, so another favorite thing of mine is roller skating. Andie hates it when I get to choose our girls' night out. She loves to bar hop, but I love to relive my childhood. We're usually the oldest people at the rink, but I make her go from time to time."

I laugh and imagine her and her friend roller-skating with a bunch of teenie boppers. It's a cute visual. "Go on."

"Oh!" she blurts out. "I know what else I love!"

"Tell me," I encourage, my smile broadening.

"Christmas songs! I could listen to them all year round," she chirps happily. "Come Thanksgiving, I've already started listening to them. They make me super happy!"

Her words make me think of Dad. There at the end. When the pancreatic cancer had stolen away his laughter and happiness without much of a warning. He was a shell of nothing but pain and sadness those days before his death. But one particular night, a few days before Christmas, he demanded to hear Bing Crosby's "White Christmas." When my mom tried to pacify him into taking a nap instead, he started throwing stuff from his nightstand. I'd saved the day with my phone. Dad watched the YouTube video over and over and over again until he fell asleep.

"You got quiet. What's wrong? Are you going to sleep? I should let you sleep," she rambles.

"No," I tell her, my voice gruff with emotion. "Go on. I was just thinking about my dad is all."

Instead of continuing, she gets quiet. "You miss him a lot. I can tell."

"I don't think I'll ever stop missing him," I admit. "He was very involved in our lives until cancer poisoned him and then stole him from us. I'll always think about him and his obsession with Bing Crosby's 'White Christmas.'" My smile is back.

"He sounds lovely," she murmurs.

I clear my throat. "Okay, what's next?"

"Hmmm, I also love winter. It's the best season of the year. I love the holidays. I love the snow. I love the giving spirit of everyone around us. I love that I can wear leggings, oversized sweaters, and boots every day." She sighs with happiness. "I just love it."

I imagine a pretty brunette with rosy cheeks laughing as snowflakes dot her hair and cheeks. "I like winter, too," I tell her absently.

"Also, I love *ER*. Do you remember that show? I have all the box sets and anytime I'm on vacation from work or bored or lonely or sad, I watch *ER*. Every time, I get sucked in and forget the world around me."

"You're cute," I blurt out.

"Daryl didn't think so," she murmurs, a bitter tone in her voice. "Can you believe I gave that guy nearly a year of my life? He did me so wrong…and yet…" she trails off and huffs. "I still feel bad. Like I was the one who broke up with him. I mean, I technically did, I guess. But I feel like it's my fault we ended. Because had I not seen him sucking face with his neighbor, we'd still be together."

Jealousy flares in my chest, but I quickly quell it down. "Were you happy with him?"

"Not exactly," she says sadly. "But I wasn't lonely either."

"You're not alone now," I remind her. "Three more favorite things. Spill, Buttercup."

She laughs. "Mr. Impatient. Okay, so, um...maybe that's it. Maybe I don't have anymore favorite things."

"Big liar," I tease. "You're one of those people who loves everything. You find something positive and good about any single thing, besides assholes like Daryl, and try to like something out of it. Am I right?"

She groans and then huffs. "Andie says I'm too nice."

"Since when did nice become a bad thing?" I question. "You just need someone who appreciates and doesn't take advantage of your niceness. Being nice is a good quality to have. Now tell me three more things."

"You're nice too, Ram," she whispers. Her sweet voice sends tremors of need rippling through me. "I love...oh my God...I don't even know how to say this without sounding like a total weirdo."

I snort. "Now I need to know. And, by the way, I love how you say the words 'oh my God' just as dramatically as when you text them."

Her giggles are soothing. "Okay, fine. I love folding towels. Isn't that strange? I mean, who admits to that? Towels! That's weird. Nobody loves to do laundry. That's the most boring thing ever. But truth is, Andie has had to drag me out of JC Penney's before because I got stuck folding all their towels so they'd look neat. They were an awful mess! I couldn't stand to look at them so I started folding them all. I even had a couple of people ask me questions where certain items were in the store because they thought I worked there. Of course, I shop there a lot so I was able to direct them, this, also, to Andie's horror."

She starts giggling so hard I think she's crying. It makes me chuckle too.

"I want to see you," I say. It just comes out. "God, how I want to see you."

She grows quiet. "Maybe one day. I'd like to keep getting to know each other first."

"Fine," I grumble in faux annoyance. "Two more, towel girl."

"Let's see…oh! I know one. I absolutely love cheese. Oh my God!! Cheese is the best thing ever. Like, I could eat it on everything probably. Sometimes I even ask the restaurant I'm eating at to melt a piece of cheese on my steak. Andie says that is, and I quote, 'fuckin' disgusting,' but I can't help it. It's soooo good. I'm going to go to a cheese factory one day in Wisconsin. I'll watch how it's made and then take home a whole trunkful of cheese." She groans and huffs again. "Gah, I just rambled some more. What is it with you that gives me verbal diarrhea? Ew, that's gross. Diarrhea and cheese don't belong in the same sentence." Then, she gags.

I start laughing so hard, I nearly drop my phone. "Y-You're t-too much," I manage to get out between breaths.

She growls like the cutest goddamned kitten ever. "It *IS* gross, Ram!"

"L-Last thing," I stammer out as I try to contain my laughter.

More of that breathy frustration on her end that gets my cock hard. "Fine. Okay, last thing." The line goes quiet. "I love old people."

"Old people?"

"I know, I know," she utters. "Laugh all you want but it's true. When I was sixteen, they took my choir class to sing at an old folks' home. My grandparents on both sides were both dead by the time I was old enough to remember them, so I never really hung out with old people. But man, this old folks' home was full of them. Some were really sad. Their eyes were hollow. It made my heart hurt for them. But then, some were hilarious. They'd regale you with tales from their youth. The old men would flirt like it was no big deal. The old ladies would gush about how pretty you were. It was just fun. Old people are fun. Then, after high school, I would volunteer at the home sometimes. I'd cry when some of my favorites would die. But mostly, I did a lot of laughing. And, man oh man, those old people are serious about their board games. Scrabble and I came together as a set when I'd visit. There was always someone there who wanted to play with me." She lets out a sigh. "That's it. Ten nerdy things about me. I bet you think I'm the weirdest woman you've ever met."

"Actually," I tell her, my voice husky. "I think you're beautiful."

She screeches on the other line. "You haven't seen me, though! How could you possibly think I'm beautiful? What if I'm not your type? What if you don't like my nose or my hair or my eyes? What if I'm too skinny for you or not skinny enough? What if you think my perfume smells like something you hate? What if—"

I cut her off. "What if I don't care about any of that? I think you are beautiful. I didn't say your face or your body. I said you. And of course that sexy-as-sin hand, but mostly you. You're funny and sweet and a little on the oddball side but that's what makes you beautiful."

When I hear sniffling on the other end, I feel guilty. I've made her cry. Dammit!

"That's the nicest thing anyone besides my best friend has ever said to me," she says, her voice wobbly. "I don't know what to say."

"You say thank you and accept it as truth. Fuckers like Daryl didn't appreciate you. Fuckers like me do though. And I can't wait to know more."

She sniffles again. "I need to go. Early day tomorrow."

God, I wish I were there to swipe away her tears for her. "I don't want you to go."

She laughs and it's good to know her crying has subsided. "I have to."

"Call me next time you get lonely. I'll always answer if I can."

"Thank you," she says sweetly. "Goodnight, Ram."

"Night, Buttercup."

We hang up and an instant feeling of loss overwhelms me. I stare up at the darkened ceiling for a whole ten minutes without moving. Instead of thinking about my insecurities and past, I think about her. I replay all of her stories in my head again. She's so vibrant and colorful. Life drips from her and I want to drink it all up. I've known the woman but a couple of days and I'm quickly becoming obsessed with her. If Roman knew how wrapped up I was in this unidentified stranger, he'd slap some sense into me. And that's exactly why he doesn't get to know. I want to keep moving forward. Senseless is fun.

My phone starts vibrating on my chest. When I see it's Carrie, I grin as I answer.

"That was quick," I tell her with a chuckle.

"Remember how you said we could be brave over the phone? Because we don't know each other?" Her voice is serious, if not strained.

"Yeah."

"I started to touch myself after we hung up but..." she trails off. My dick thickens at the mere thought of her fingers under her panties.

"But what?"

"But it's more exhilarating to talk to you while I do it. Oh my God," she whispers. "That's so embarrassing to admit. I'm glad I can't see your face judging me."

A growl rumbles through me. "I'm definitely not judging. I'm imagining that sexy little thumb with the chipped, navy blue polish and your other finger pinching your clit. It's not judging, babe. It's hot as fuck."

She lets out a whimper. "Hearing you talk like that is hot too."

"I could talk you right through your embarrassment. What do you say?"

I can hear her swallow. "Okay."

Sitting up, I run my fingers through my messy hair. My heart is thundering in my chest and my cock is straining against my sweatpants. "What are you wearing?"

"A big T-shirt and some panties," she tells me bravely.

"Take them off," I order, my voice a low growl.

She shuffles around and then she squeaks out a "done."

"Good girl. Now, I want you to touch your right nipple and tell me what you feel," I instruct. My own hand tugs my sweatpants down my thighs until my heavy cock bobs out. Gripping it, I wait for her to speak.

"Um, the nipple is hard. My nipples are small. I have little boobs," she complains.

"I like little boobs," I encourage. My dick jolts at the idea of coming all over her pretty little tits.

"Oh, good," she murmurs. "Um, I'm aching. Down there."

"Down where?"

"There."

"Your cunt?"

"Oh my God!" she shrieks. "You said the C-word!"

I laugh as I stoke my dick. "Don't tell me you can't say cunt."

"It's awful, Ram. The worst bad word ever," she hisses.

"Say cunt, Buttercup."

"Nope. Not saying it out loud," she grumbles.

"We'll continue this conversation later. Until then, slip your hand down to your pussy. Is pussy a better word?" I question with a grin.

She giggles. "It's better. Okay, I'm touching it."

"Your clit."

"Mmmmhmmm."

Her breathy voice, coupled with knowing she's touching her clit, has me closing my eyes. I fill in the blanks with Carrie by using the brunette from the bar, Dani, in my fantasy. In my head, she's lying on my bed with her brown hair decorating the pillow beneath her. Her small tits jiggle as she squirms each time she touches her clit.

"Spread your thighs, baby," I coo. My hand fists my cock harder. "I want you to tell me if your cunt is wet. Are you dripping for me?"

She moans, and I nearly spill my seed right then.

Slowing my fisting, I wait for her to answer. Finally, "Yes. I'm wet. Very wet actually. In fact," she rambles, "I have never been this wet, I don't think."

My cock aches for release. "You'll only ever get that wet for me," I growl. For some reason, I feel that vow down to my very being. "Rub your slick finger all over your clit. And when you think you might come, Buttercup, I want you to stick that finger in your mouth. Since I'm not there, it's only fair you tell me how good you taste."

She moans louder this time. Her breaths come out ragged and uneven. Then, I hear a sucking sound. "I taste strange."

"I bet you taste like you and you already know how much I like you. One day I'm going to taste you for myself. What do you think about that?" I mumble, my fist moving quicker over my length.

"I'm scared. What if we don't get on in person?"

"We'll get on. So well, in fact, that I can guarantee you that the moment we actually meet in the flesh, I'll have my tongue down your throat within the first ten minutes. And you'll be begging for much more than that," I tell her with a growl.

She moans again and I know she's back to fingering herself. With her soft breaths in my ear, I go quiet as I focus on my cock.

"One day soon, I am going to suck on your clit for you, Buttercup. I'm going to bite it until you beg me not to. You'll come all over my tongue, and when I taste you, I'll confirm that you don't taste strange at all. I bet you taste sweet like honey," I murmur.

"Oh, God," she gasps. And then a long moan of

pleasure. My own climax jolts through me. Heat from my release splashes my stomach, and I let out a groan of relief. When we both come down from our highs, the air feels different.

Whoever you are, Buttercup, I'm coming for you.

"Thank you, Ram." She sighs happily. "That was weird if I think about it too hard. But I don't want to think of it as weird. I loved it. It's okay to admit that, right? I'm not a skank if that's what you're thinking. I've never done this before."

I shake my head and grin. "You're not a skank. You're mine."

We hang up not long after and for the first time in months, I sleep.

Chapter Seven

Dani

> **Time to Pay the Piper**

"**Y**OU HAVE *GOT* TO BE KIDDING ME HERE," ANDIE says in an exasperated tone. "Again?"

"What?"

I've barely just walked into work at the bank and Andie is all up on me. I look to see if I have something on my shirt.

"Not your damn shirt," she groans. "Your smile." She pulls a face as if smiling is a bad thing. "Really, Dani? Another?"

I begin to blush at what she's getting at. I should have never told her about the first one.

"This is getting ridiculous. We're on day five of you and that goofy-ass weird I-did-strange-things-over-the-phone-with-a-guy look." Her lip curls up as if this is the oddest thing she's ever heard of.

I bring my hands to my cheeks. Do I look weird? I don't feel like I look any different. Maybe a constant smile rests on my face more lately, but that's a given. The past five days with Ram have been…perfect. My cheeks and throat heat as I think about just how perfect my late night calls with him have been.

"Oh God, you're thinking about it right now, aren't you? I'm going to vomit. Ew," Andie says and starts making fake gagging noises.

I ignore her jesting and set my purse under my teller booth. For the past five days, Ram and I have talked. A lot. We've gotten to know more about one another, in a way that I don't think I ever have with any other boyfriend.

Oh my God! I just compared him to a boyfriend.

Friend.

He's a friend.

But then again, do friends do what we've been scantily doing all week?

My cheeks must be blazing crimson at this point. I pick at the polish on my nail and let my hair curtain around my face as I hide the evidence of my naughty ways from Andie and all my other coworkers.

Each night our conversations have led us both into a heated craze. One thing ends up leading to another, and then we're both touching ourselves, talking through every move like we're lying in the same bed. As if we're actually touching each other.

Quite frankly, it's hot.

Exhilarating and exciting.

And fun.

But it's more than that. It's almost as if I know him

already and he hasn't even set eyes on me. It's strange, though. Sometimes, during his heated praises, the way he compliments me, it's like he already knows me.

And Lord help me. The things he says. Naughty. Dirty. Straight up bad. Vulgar words that cause me to turn bright red with embarrassment, but at the same time, gush with wetness between my legs.

I like it.

I like him.

I like what we've been doing.

"That's it! I'm pulling my desperate card." I break from my thoughts to look at Andie, who's manhandling the money till into her drawer.

"What's *it*? And what's a desperate card?" I ask, confusion making my nose scrunch. "What is this look you're giving me?"

"It's my, '*I'm sick of watching you walk in those doors every morning with that I just did naughty things to myself with a complete stranger over the phone*' look. I need to get laid. And I'm pulling my desperate card."

I giggle at her, still not following. "I never said I was doing anything over the phone, besides that one time, and I still don't understand the desperate card."

"Oh bullshit!" she bellows. "You've been practically skipping in here each morning. You actually said no to Frank yesterday about picking up his shift, *without* me coaching you, and dammit, even your skin looks better. You're getting it. In some way, shape, or form."

I start to laugh at her outburst. I only admitted to Andie the first time and that was enough for me. The shock, then laughter, then drilling me to give her all the details was enough for me to keep the second, and the third…and the fourth to myself.

"I will plead the fifth on all of that," I tell her with a coy smile. "Besides the Frank thing. He was crazy to think that since I wouldn't cover his shift that I would take his dog again to the vet. No and no."

"I know, girl, and sweet move on making him pay you right then and there for the last vet visit. My jaw about fell off, listening to you demand he pay you that moment or that you would take it up with management." She flashes me a grin full of pride.

I smile to myself as well. Ever since talking to Ram, there's been this change in me. Confidence maybe? He just says such kind things to me. Makes me feel…I don't know. Important? During one of our nightly chats, I went into telling him about the pushover side of me, about how I let Daryl walk all over me, and even about the money I lent him. He got angry for me but then tried to coach me, just as Andie did, on how to say no. It turned into a game of sexual banter, and while the beginning started with me teasing myself, telling him no, it ended with me panting "yes, yes, yes."

"I can't. I just don't have it in me to say that. It's just… just… mean," I say at the bold statement Ram is coaching me to say when I confront Daryl, which he has convinced me is a must *to get my money back.*

"Buttercup, it's not mean. It's the truth. That asshole fucked you over and ripped you off. You should rip off his balls."

My heart warms at my nickname. He is right, though. Daryl cannot get away with taking that money from me.

"Okay fine. I'll say it, but I'm not sure about the whole breaking things part."

"Then fuck his office up somehow. Does he have furniture in there? Take a knife or a key to it. Just get all crazy badass so he knows you mean business." He finishes his statement on a laugh. We both know I don't have an ounce of badass crazy in me. I've changed out of my work clothes into a thin tank top and panties. I crawl into bed, making myself more comfortable.

"You got a bit quiet. Tell me what you're doing right now." His voice is deep, his request more of a statement.

I push away the thin sheet covering from the hip down and kick it the rest of the way off. Then, I allow my thumb to graze my skin, the feeling of being touched while hearing his voice, enthralling. *"I just got into bed. I was making myself cozy."*

His grunt at knowing exactly what I'm doing despite my lies does this to me. It makes me so hot for him. Every time this week that we've started something past a casual conversation, it's begun with me letting him know my position.

"Fuck, FaceTime me. Please. Let me see you."

I laugh, brushing my fingers along my navel and lower stomach. *"No! What if I have hairy legs and I didn't shave. You would run for the hills. Plus...I'm not ready for that."*

"God, Buttercup, when you are..." he trails off and lets out a rush of breath. *"I swear I'm going to do things to you that will change you."*

His words are like sexual triggers for me. No man has ever had such a tongue like Ram does. The things he says to me. The promises he makes. My hand moves up my stomach gently squeezing my breast. I feel so naughty touching myself while he talks, but the past few days have taught me a boldness I never knew I had.

"Your breathing is picking up," he murmurs, his voice thick with lust. "Are you touching yourself, Buttercup?"

I am.

And I wish his hands were on my skin, caressing my breasts, pinching my hardened nipples, stroking the wetness that's building between my thighs.

"Answer me, fuck." He groans, and I wonder if he's touching himself too. "I can tell you're touching yourself. It's making me grip my cock, hearing those little gusts of air. Where are your hands, Buttercup?"

His questions spark another wave of desire, knowing how naughty I am for admitting it. But I do. "I'm touching my breast. Squeezing my nipple, because it's hard and sensitive with arousal."

His growl of approval is like heaven to me. He doesn't think I'm skanky or insane for what I'm doing. He's loving it. I move my hand across my chest to my other breast and offer the same sensual torment. This causes my eyes to shut, my pelvis lifting from the bed, begging to be touched.

"I'm stroking my cock, wishing it were your hand," he mutters, his voice low and sensual. "Your smooth skin stroking me up and down."

Oh, God. That visual is almost my undoing. I bet his cock is thick and long and veiny and perfect. I'm willing to bet he knows how to use it too.

"So perfect," he murmurs.

At his words I pinch my nipple harder, allowing a soft moan to escape my lips. His voice is like an aphrodisiac for me, turning my senses wild. Feeling bolder than I have the past few nights, I release my breast and work my hand back down my stomach to my aching center. I dip through my trimmed hair and, automatically, my fingers are saturated. "Oh God, I'm already so wet," I tell him, breathless. "My fingers are soaked."

Another groan from his end. "Fuck, babe, if I were there, I would use my tongue to suck you up and eat your eager pussy. Put your finger inside you. Pretend it's my finger and tell me how much you want it to be me."

I moan at his dirty words, but I do as I'm told. I lower my hand using my middle finger to caress my folds, then push one finger inside me.

"Oh yes, that feels so good. So good," I repeat as I pull out and push back inside. I can hear Ram panting along with me. I know he is just as lost as I am while he works his cock.

"That's it," he instructs, his voice a gravelly whisper. "Now I want you to put two fingers inside that tight pussy of yours."

My sex gushes with arousal at his demand. I do as he says, once again, and work two fingers inside me. The feeling is filling and wonderful. I can't help but work them in and out as I wait for my release.

That's what his words do to me.

They make me lose control.

Turn me on.

Make me wild.

"Oh God, Ram, this feels so good. I'm going to come soon."

I hear his breathing pick up, and I know he's working

himself harder and faster. The thought of me being with him, watching him as I work his cock with my hands and mouth, throws me into a spiral of desire. "Oh God, I'm going to… I'm going to—"

"Three fingers, Buttercup," he barks out with an animalistic growl. "Fill yourself. I want you to know how it would feel if I was fucking you. I want you to feel stretched and full with my cock."

It's then I shove three fingers inside me and explode.

"Any who," Andie chirps. "We're going out tonight."

I shake off the memory, hoping my face isn't flushed simply from remembering.

Bringing my attention back to my best friend, I let out a sigh. "I don't know if I can." I think about how much I look forward to my chats with Ram and our intimate moments. Going out means I'll miss that.

"Oh, yes we are. You're coming with me," she tells me with a sly grin. "We're going to Bender's. And I'm going to proposition Brett."

At that I choke on my gum. I start coughing and it takes Andie to beat on my back for me to cough up the piece of gum. "You what!?"

"Yeah, you heard me. He's a hot piece of meat and he's nice to us. He looks like he can toss a girl around too, and I need it. Dani, I am *dying* here! I need ass. I need to scream a random dude's name. Well, in this scenario, it will be Brett's."

Brett has been nothing but awesome since we started going to Bender's regularly but, to be honest, he kind of scares me. He's just so big and biker-ish. "What if he's into tons of scary stuff? Ties you up and gags you?"

Andie shrugs her shoulders. "At this point, fine by me."

"Andie!"

"What? I'm serious. And like you're one to judge. You're having phone sex with a complete stranger *who* you've never met. At least I know Brett is an actual person." She arches a blonde eyebrow as if waiting for me to challenge her.

And that's just the thing. Ram *does* want to meet. But I keep finding ways to avoid, make excuses, or simply say no.

With each pleading text message, he bargains with something close to unbearable to resist. I remember the first one that came through after our "favorite things" conversation.

> **Ram: Meet me for a drink. Coffee. Anything. I think it's time we start doing this in person.**
>
> **Me: I can't. I'm really busy. Plus I'm not ready.**
>
> **Ram: I'm dying over here. Don't make me beg.**
>
> **Me: Begging can be a good thing. I'm just not sure about this yet. What if you're not real? I like us how we are now.**

And that message was the truth. What if he wasn't who he truly seemed to be on the phone? And on our texts? What if this was an act and the second we met he turned into a rude, cheating jerk? I didn't want to compare him to Daryl. I just couldn't fully let my guard down, afraid of getting hurt again. He dropped it until the next night, after our second inappropriate phone call ended.

Ram: FaceTime me at least.

Me: No.

Ram: I'll buy you a pony if you FaceTime me.

Me: No.

Ram: I'll take you to Silver Dollar City so you can sing Christmas carols and eat taffy.

Me: Super tempting, but no.

Ram: If you FaceTime me, I will spread cheese all over my naked body and you can picture licking it all off me.

At that I laughed, picturing a good soft Brie cheese-spread smeared all over his beautiful chest. And of course the heat spread across my face as I imagined doing what he offered. Me. Licking him clean. One cheesy inch at a time.

"Well, for your information he *does* want to meet me," I reply, sticking my chin up.

"And you haven't? Why? Besides the whole possible could be a serial killer theory."

I toss a pad of Post-its at her. "He's not a serial killer. He's sweet and kind. He's easy to talk to—"

"And masturbate off to?" Andie chuckles as another pad goes flying her way. "What!? It's just a question. I mean if he's giving you all this phone pleasure, then why not test out the real thing? I mean come on… Guys can only hold off for so long. Sooner or later, you're gonna have to pay the piper."

My forehead creases as I quickly tie my hair up in a

bun before it gets busy. "And what exactly is *that* supposed to mean?"

"You know. You continue to talk to him, and you tease him with your sexy phone words and panting, *NOT* that I know what you sound like, ew, but still... sooner or later, you're going to have to say yes and meet him or cut ties. Meet him in person and do the real deed or move on. Either way, you're going to have to choose."

The conversation is dropped because the morning rush kicks in, breaking up our discussion. But her words eat at me. If I don't decide, and possibly offer to meet, then he might pull away and assume I'm not worth the trouble. Maybe Andie *is* right. It might be time to put my big girl pants on and pay that piper.

Chapter Eight

Ram

> ### Bartender My Ass

Me: Why are you so opposed to FaceTime anyway? You could Skype instead on your computer. Just cut off your head if that makes you feel better. At least I'd be able to watch you when you touch yourself…

Smirking, I climb out of my car and trot toward the bank to open my new business account. Wind whips around me and some ice pellets sting my face. The weather is attempting to get shitty the closer it gets to Christmas, but I'm smiling like a dumbass because I know it'll make Carrie happy. Between the Christmas and the snow, she'll be thrilled.

She doesn't respond right away, but I'm not too worried. I push through the bank doors and groan when I see it's jam packed with people. Luckily, one customer service rep is just thanking a customer who is leaving. I walk over to him and plop down. While he helps me set up the business account with the check Inigo Photog wrote me, I let my mind wander to the past week. Each night, we've pretty much had phone sex. It's been so fucking hot. I need her in the flesh. What's been playful banter is barely hiding my raging desire to have her truly naked and beneath me. Unfortunately, she's not biting. I think she likes our perfect little bubble and is afraid to destroy it. To me, it doesn't matter what she looks like. I already like her a lot. She doesn't have to be pretty. She could be missing teeth or have warts on her nose. I don't care. It's her soft sighs. Her sweet laughs. Her corny jokes. All of that is what draws me to her. Looks aren't everything.

"Would you like any other signers on your account?" the customer service rep named Jack asks.

"Probably my brother but I can add him later. We'll just set it up this way for now," I instruct.

He taps away and has me sign a few documents. I've been loaded down with a folder full of paperwork and a temporary book of checks. When he rises from his seat to deposit the check at the teller line, I hear it.

A voice.

Familiar.

It draws me to it like a moth seeking a flame.

"Here you go, Mr. Sorenson. Extra sugar because you're so bitter," the sweet voice chirps.

An old man chuckles behind me. "You'd think as an investor at this bank, I'd get special treatment. Not from you, Miss Danielle."

The woman giggles and it's so fucking cute I have to

turn around. I've got to put a face to the voice.

"You *did* get special treatment," she admonishes, her tone playful. "Look at that line. I stepped away from the teller line to get your spoiled tail some coffee."

Their backs are turned to me and the white-headed old man pats the tiny woman on the back. Her dark brown hair has been piled into a messy bun. She wears an oversized cream sweater that seems to swallow her tiny frame. And brown leggings hug her slender thighs. She wears a pair of heeled knee-high boots and shifts her weight back and forth on them. It makes me wonder what her ass looks like hiding under her sweater.

"I really need to get back before they fire me," she urges, a chuckle in her voice.

The old man has a gentle grip on her elbow. "You tell those old coots if they fire you, I'll fire them. I'll take my money and give it to whichever bank you end up at."

They both laugh and I feel awkward eavesdropping. But not awkward enough that I don't get up and take several steps over to them. Careful not to be too obvious, I walk in front of them over to the coffee machine. Glittering hazel eyes meet mine for a brief moment. Recognition flickers in her eyes.

It's Dani.

The girl Roman knocked over at the bar the other day.

My heart skips a couple of beats as I greedily drink her in. Her pouty pink lips are curved into a shy smile that has my dick reacting against my wishes. God, this girl is hot. And seeing her twice within a week is not a coincidence.

I should ask her out.

But as soon as the thought enters my brain, I squash

it. I couldn't do that to Carrie. We're basically having sex, even if we haven't physically done the deed, and I owe it to her to see how it plays out.

When Dani's cheeks redden, I wink at her. I can't help it. She's too fucking cute. And when she turns impossibly more crimson, I grin at her, flashing her my panty-melting smile I know works on just about any chick.

She turns away and shakes her head as if to get me out of her mind.

"Mr. Holloway," Jack says as he hands me a receipt. "You're all good. Thanks for opening your business account with us. Please call if you have any questions or concerns."

I give him a nod and steal another glance at Dani.

"Go home, Mr. Sorenson," Dani chides the old man. "Don't make me call your wife."

His laughter bellows, but I'm frozen in spot. That voice. I *knew* I recognized it. She waves to the old man and starts back over to the teller line where people are standing around impatiently. I just gape after her.

No fucking way.

"She's a real catch," the old man tells me, pointing at Dani. "If I was fifty years younger..." He whistles and waggles his white eyebrows at me. "But a young chap like yourself? You'd be lucky to marry a girl like that. They don't come any sweeter and they certainly don't come any prettier."

When she gets back to her window, she begins working quickly, never losing her perfect smile. I take a deep breath and hurry out of the building before I do something stupid like crawl over the countertop and kiss her like mad in front of the entire lobby. Instead, I trot out to my car and plop down in my seat.

Bartender my ass.

I pull out my phone. She hasn't responded to my last text and it's clear to see why. She's busy and it isn't slinging drinks.

Me: Have dinner with me. I'd say lunch but I have a meeting with a potential new client. Please. I just need to see you again.

With a chuckle, I toss my phone down and put the car in drive. She'll probably think it was a typo. There's no way she put together me as the same guy from the bar. No more hiding. I'm smiling as I drive deeper into the city. This whole time I imagined "Carrie's" face to be that of Dani. Each time I jerked off with her sweet voice in my ear. Each time I fantasized about her lying naked next to me in bed. And now, I realize it's true. They are one in the same. The thought is exhilarating.

I swing by the house for a bit to change into something more professional and to gather some printed off material for the new potential client. During that time, I take a call from Roman. He checks in on how everything is going with my business. I find it odd he's so interested in the day-to-day operations. When I get a minute, I'm going to shake him down and figure out what's going on with him. Two hours later, and I'm sitting in a chair outside Mr. Winston's office.

Dani still hasn't replied back. I'm staring at my phone when I hear screaming. The receptionist makes eye contact with me and rolls her eyes.

"Trouble follows him," she tells me in a bored tone.

My anxiety causes my chest to tighten. I was hoping for a good client. Not an asshole.

"You are the worst person ever!" a woman shrieks.

I lean to the side to have a better listen through the door.

"Give it to me. Give me the key," a man says.

"GIVE ME MY TEN GRAND, YOU PRICK!"

"You lent it to me!" he roars back.

Something about the way he talks to the woman has my hackles rising. I'm already on my feet, starting toward the door.

"Oh, mister," she bites out, her voice losing some of its fire. "I'm about to give you your stupid key."

I hear her grunting through the door.

"Why won't it cut?" she hollers.

"It's real leather, dingbat," the man snaps back. "You can't cut it with a key."

I smirk when I hear the key hit what sounds like a glass surface with a clang. Then I hear glass crashing.

"But I can break that stupid vase by throwing it to the floor!" she hollers in triumph. "And this plant," she cackles. "Dead!" Another crash.

"You've lost your mind," he bellows. "This isn't like you!"

She lets out a choked sound, and for a moment, I wonder if she's going to cry. "You made me this way," she bites out in a cold tone. "Call me when you have my money. You have one week or I'll do something worse. Way worse. Like…I'll put bologna on your car! Ha!" the woman threatens.

Bologna?

"Listen…" he gripes out. "Just fucking listen."

"No, buddy," she snips. "You listen to me. Money. One week. Bye."

I'm caught eavesdropping when the door slings open and the woman slams right into my chest. The first thing I notice is the sweet scent of a perfume I don't recognize. I inhale it because I like how it smells. My eyes find my client's. He's an older guy with a receding hairline and a slight belly. How he got this cute tiny little thing is beyond me.

"Is that your new boyfriend?" Mr. Winston hisses. "You sure moved on quick. So unlike you, Dani."

Dani.

Holy fuck.

A shit-eating grin stretches across my face and my chest momentarily tightens.

The woman—who I now realize is Dani—attempts to peel herself away from me. I didn't realize I'd naturally locked my arms around her. Her head tilts up and she regards me with those hazel eyes that are now red and teary. A possessive growl rumbles in my throat.

This isn't just a coincidence. This is something way damn bigger. Sure, our town isn't that huge, but seeing her twice in one day *is* unfuckingbelievable. Each of our paths have led to the same place. Exactly where we're supposed to be.

Upon realizing this asshole just spouted some nasty shit to my girl, my smile falls and I glare at him. "She dated down for you, dude," I snap, not caring that I'll lose this client. I don't want to do business with his fucking cheating ass anyway. "Clearly, you let something perfect slip right out of your hands. Don't worry, asshole," I growl. "I'm going to take *real* good care of her."

She stiffens in my arms but stops trying to escape my grip. I wave my middle finger at the loser before tucking her under my arm and stalking out of the office. Once we're outside, the wind attempts to blow us away. It's cold as fuck out here. Dani lets me guide her over to where, apparently, our two cars are the only ones parked in the lot. I push her hips back until her ass meets the side door of her car.

"Dani." All I say is her name and she's looking up at me in awe. Her pink lips are parted in surprise. The same pink lips I've fantasized sucking on my cock. God, she's so beautiful.

"Y-You—" she chatters out, confusion marring her perfect features. "It's really you? The guy from the bar? From the bank? *You're Ram*? My stranger-danger Ram. I can't believe this."

I beam at her, mostly because she called me *her* Ram, and I rub my hands up and down the sides of her arms. The sweater isn't warm enough for this weather. I attempt to block the wind from her and press my hard body against her soft one. Sliding my fingers into her messy hair, I tilt her face up so I can inspect every part of her. She does the same, her hazel eyes darting all over me but lingering on my mouth.

"Buttercup," I murmur. "It's me. All me."

She doesn't try to wriggle away when I draw closer to her. "But how? This is all so overwhelming."

"Don't get overwhelmed, gorgeous." Nudging my nose

against her ice cold one, I shrug. "Too many signs from the universe to ignore, though." My hands crave to touch every part of her. I settle for leaving them weaved into her silky hair. "I'm going to kiss you now," I tell her, my tone smug.

A small whine, one I remember hearing just last night right before she came, escapes her. "Here? Right now?" she protests, but not too hard. "What if someone sees?"

I smile. "Let them fucking see."

My lips brush across hers and her breath hitches. I don't wait for any more permission. Her heaving breathing, parted lips, and death grip on my leather jacket are enough to have me forging ahead. As soon as our tongues touch, she lets out a whimper. So needy and hungry. She tastes like lingering coffee with a mix of peppermint. Her taste reminds me of Christmas. I almost chuckle, realizing that she'd like that analogy.

With a groan, I deepen our kiss. Her kiss, while unsure at first, begins to greedily dance with mine. The shock has worn off and given in to the desire that surely matches mine. Our kiss is wet and noisy and hot as hell. When she moans again and tilts her head back as if to break our kiss, I move on to the shell of her ear. I whisper how beautiful she is before sucking on her ear lobe. She gasps in pleasure. My lips find the soft flesh of her neck and I suckle the sweet skin there. An overwhelming desire to mark her washes over me. I suck a little harder on her and her fingers tangle into my hair. My hands are eager to roam all over her, but I don't want to scare her away. I simply want to kiss and hold her. For now.

"Oh my God…" she moans, her fingers tugging at my

hair. "This is real. You're real. You're…"

I nip at her flesh before licking away the sting. "Say it. Say my name again," I breathe against the vein in her throat that is pumping like mad.

"Ram!"

My hands ignore the desire to remain a gentleman and I slip them around to her backside under her sweater. She has a nice ass hiding in those leggings. I grab on to it and my sweet little thing jumps slightly. Understanding washes over me and I lift her like she wants. Her slender legs hook around my waist. I lift my head from her throat so I can look at her. Those hazel eyes are blazing with lust. When I grind my hardened cock against her soft center, her eyes roll back and she cries out.

"Oh my God," she whines, her head turns to the side and she darts her gaze for onlookers. "I don't do this sort of thing. Not with a stranger. Not in public."

I give her a wolfish grin. "You do now. Besides, I thought you were working on being brave, baby. I call what we're doing really fuckin' brave."

Her smile is shy, but it matches my own. It draws me back to her like a magnet until we're once again hot and heavy. It's not enough, though, I crave more of her.

And then I'm rubbing against her in a way that's too sinful for public and she's not saying no anymore. She wants this, too. There are probably eyes everywhere and I don't even care. Apparently, she's throwing caution to the wind too. I want to make her come right here. Right now. I don't even care if I come in my own slacks doing it. Anything to hear that soft whine she makes when she loses control.

She jerks her head to the left this time and looks for anyone watching. I murmur in her ear that it's just us. My hot breath seems to excite her because then our mouths are once again latched.

My cock seems to know exactly how to rub against her because it situates to fit between the lips of her pussy. Each time I grind against her, she makes louder and louder noises as it slides against her clit. The wind whips around us, but I'm not even cold anymore. And judging by the way she's clawing at my shoulders now and rocking with me, neither is she.

I don't even try to stop myself when one hand leaves her ass and slips up under her sweater. She moans when I grab her tit through her bra. They're small, like she says, but so perfect in my hand. I'm just working my thumb under the material to touch her nipple when she lets out one of her telling whines.

"Just us," I assure her. "You're so fucking brave, Buttercup."

And so close. Another few moments and she'll unravel.

I massage her pebbled nipple while I thrust against her. My mouth steals kisses and occasionally takes little bites of her neck. With a choked murmur of my name, she comes hard. Her entire body quakes and I can't wait for her to do it when I'm buried deep inside of her. I brush my lips against hers again, kissing her softly.

"Oh my God," she groans. "I can't believe I just did that. In public. With a stranger." Then she lets out a slight giggle. "In front of my ex-boyfriend's building."

"Well, I'm not a stranger anymore, Dani." I like her

name on my tongue. I especially like her on my tongue. I chuckle. "Believe it, though. We're going to do more of it later, too. Next time in private." I pull back so I can stare at her stunning flushed face. Her legs are still locked around my waist and my dick is aching for release, but I remain still as I regard her. "You're fucking gorgeous, Buttercup."

Her eyes light up and she beams at me just as someone yells.

"I called the cops, Dani!" Mr. Winston bellows. "I knew you were losing your damn mind! You're outta control!"

The growl rumbling from me is fierce. I set her on her feet and reluctantly peel myself away from her. When I stalk over to the goofy-looking asshole, he stumbles away from me. I clutch his tie and yank him so I can get right in his face.

"Talk to my girlfriend one more time in that tone and I'll shove my fist up your ass. Comprende, motherfuck-er?" My teeth are clenched as I glower at him.

"Uh...uh..." he stammers, fear glimmering in his eyes. "I understand."

With a snarl, I shove him away from me. "And I suggest you give my woman her money back as she asks or I'll be forced to come extract it from you."

He backs away shaking his head. "I'll get her the money. Jesus!"

Turning away from him, I trot back over to Dani. She's staring at me as if I'm some mystical creature...and she hasn't even seen my cock yet.

"Come on," I tell her, grabbing her hand. "Let's get

you out of this cold. When I pick you up after work, you better wear something warmer."

She laughs as I all but stuff her back into her car. Before I close the door, I lean in and steal another sweet kiss. "Who says we're going to see each other after work?" she questions, her lips curving into a breathtaking smile.

"I do. I'm taking you on a date. We have to make up for lost time," I tell her with a smirk.

Fear flashes in her eyes briefly as if her mind just worked out the fact that we've finally met. Her stranger is a stranger no more.

"Turn off that mind of yours," I growl and lean forward into her car. "This is a good thing," I assure her. "Let it happen." I kiss her again.

She still seems unconvinced, so I convince her. My palm finds her thigh and I slip my fingers over her pussy through her leggings. I know she's still sensitive from her recent orgasm. She jolts from the touch and lets out a pleased moan.

"I'll give you more of those after I feed your sexy little ass," I vow. "You're going to need your appetite, Buttercup. We're about to work it up for sure."

Pulling away, ignoring her grumble when my hand leaves her warm thigh, I wink at her. I close the car door and watch with an ache in my chest as she composes herself and then puts the car in reverse.

I don't second-guess my actions at all, though, the moment she passes me to leave the parking lot. Her smile is bright and her eyes are twinkling. She waves like a little kid. Everything about her tugs at my insides.

Mr. Sorenson was right.

I'd be lucky to marry a girl like that. They don't come any sweeter and they certainly don't come any prettier.

Get ready, Buttercup. I'm playing for keeps.

Chapter Nine

Dani

It's Go-Time

"**O**H MY GOD!" ANDIE SHRIEKS. "WHAT happened? You've been gone forever. Did you do it? Harold was looking for you. Gah, speak!"

I walk back into the bank from my lunch break in a daze, a quirky smile on my face. I have absolutely *no* idea where to start on what just happened.

"Oh *hell* no. You're smiling. You didn't. *He* didn't. Did you get back together with him!?" Andie yelps, scaring a customer waiting in line.

"Shhh! What's your problem!?"

"You!" She points at me. "You have that look. Why? Ew, did he give you a parting orgasm?"

My eyes widen in shock, then embarrassment, and as I pick my jaw up off the ground, I tackle Andie. I jump at her, throwing my hands over her mouth. It's clear that everyone in the bank is staring at us as we cause a scene. "Shush… Shush it right now," I say, close to her face. Her eyes bore into mine, until she calms after finding humor reflecting back at her.

"Why war you miling?" she asks, her words muffled behind my hand. I wait until I know she is ready to listen and stop yelling, then release my hand from her mouth.

"I just met Ram." I smile at how strangely exciting that sentence just sounded out of my—

"Oh my God, was Ram, Daryl? Wait… I thought you went to see Daryl? OH MY GOD, was he catfishing you!?"

Dear Lord, this girl. My hand goes back over her mouth. "Control yourself," I bark.

"I can't. I'm so confused. And you're not making much sense."

"It's because I have said one sentence. Now calm down. Let me finish."

She stares at me for a final second, then nods. "Fine," she says, and I step back. I signal for her to meet me in the break room and snap at Frank to cover our absence. Andie busts out laughing at my bold demand and crudely slaps Frank on the butt while walking past him. Once we are out of earshot of the customers, she tells me to spill.

"Okay, so first off, I did go and see Daryl. It was horrible…"

My mind flits to earlier and my mouth blabs every detail without missing a beat.

Scenarios are so much easier to discuss and practice in your head than in person. Ram had convinced me that I had to stand up for myself and get my money back. And as I agreed, I just didn't know how. He had coached me on how to get all "gangsta," but he said I couldn't say please or sorry while threatening to put a cap in his ass. By the end of the night I was pumped up and after our phone call turned frantic with need, he gave me the encouragement I needed to go through with it.

Daryl had texted me earlier in the day for his key. Demanding it actually. There was no, *Hey, by the way I'm sorry for cheating, jerking you over, and taking all your savings.* Just…*I want my key back.* Feeling brave, I'd texted him back that I would come to his office on my lunch and drop it off. *Be there*, I'd ordered. I giggled at the 'be there' comment. So bossy. Well, for me anyway.

I had gone in to work and told Andie my plan. She screamed and started giving me the 'just say no' pep talk again. I was feeling good. Confident. Daryl was done walking all over me, and I was done taking it. I'd explained to Andie how Ram had given me some advice and after I told her what he suggested I do, she'd finally admitted he didn't sound like a bad guy after all. Suggesting I key his couch, though, was still a serial killer trigger she thought. I'd just shook my head and went about my day. Andie was all smiles. She had clearly been way more excited than I was about my lunch plans.

When lunchtime hit, I drove over to Daryl's office. I'd received a strange look from his secretary, who as instructed, I flipped off, which I wasn't sure why that was necessary, but Andie said it was for effect. I'd banged on his door, sucked in a gust of air, and when I walked in, I went off.

Or at least I tried.

I'd done my best to replay the lines I'd practiced with Ram. The facial expressions I'd practiced with Andie that said I meant business. And I'd held the key in my hand, just like Andie showed me, and attempted to key Daryl's leather couch, like Ram instructed. It's a shame, though. I'm a complete wimp and leather is actually very durable. So I'd settled for knocking over an expensive vase and kicking his plant.

Andie and Ram would have been so proud of me and my theatrical show. Or at least my attempt. But sadly, Daryl wasn't. He didn't take any of my threats seriously. He'd still seen me as the pushover who would end up walking out of his office with no money, and no pride.

But then the craziest thing happened. I had given up and stormed out of Daryl's office. I couldn't take any more of his cruelty. He wasn't taking me serious and I had to get out of there before I broke down. My whole superwoman cape was fluttering to the ground and I'd needed to take cover, fast. But when I threw open his door and stepped over the threshold, I fell into the arms of someone warm and strong. The scent of cologne filling my nostrils, his minty breath teasing my senses.

Daryl came barreling behind me, catching me in the arms of this stranger, making accusations and calling me horrible names. But this stranger...

He held me tight to his chest, and as I raised my eyes to meet his, it clicked. It was him.

The guy from the bar. The bank.

But then he spoke.

And I knew.

It was *him*.

Ram.

Everything else after that happened so fast. The kiss, our hasty exit. Our inappropriate, yet exhilarating—

"HOLY SHITBUCKETS! You let him hump you on the street?" Andie blurts, interrupting my unbelievable recount of the day.

I roll my eyes, knowing I wouldn't get through my whole story, without her freaking out. "Andie, it wasn't like that—"

"Public fornication. Holy shit, I can't believe you let him… He did that to… You came in public!" she finishes on a holler.

"What in the heavens is going on back here?" I attempt to cover her mouth when the booming voice of our boss, Harold, interrupts us.

"Oh I'm sorry—"

"Mr. Sphincterson," Andie says, trying not to laugh as she swats me away. I mean, who wouldn't. His last name has Sphincter in it. "Listen, Dani just got her period really bad all over her pants, and I was just trying to—"

I slap Andie on the shoulder. "I did no—"

"*And,* as I was saying, she really needs to change her…" Andie stutters for an excuse so I step in.

"I need to leave. I'm a mess. Unless you want me to—"

"No! God no," he grumbles, his face turning slightly green. "Take your… your woman problems and have the rest of the day off."

I smile widely, then quickly mask my excitement. I turn to Andie and lean in to hug her. I whisper in her ear, "Thank you." I pull away and gather my purse, exiting the bank. With a new skip in my step, I head home for my date.

With Ram.

"Where are you taking me?" I squeal, trying to keep up with him, while he grips my hand tightly in his as he maneuvers us through the busy downtown square.

"It's a surprise." He beams at me and it warms me down to my toes, even in the brisk December chill. He zig-zags us through crowds of busy shoppers and carolers, which I smile at, hoping to catch a bit of their performance on the way back, and small children giggling and enjoying the seasonal festivities.

We finally halt at the old movie theater, and as we walk up to the ticket booth, Ram pulls out his wallet, and purchases two tickets.

"*A Christmas Story*?" I ask, my voice filled with humor.

"Oh yeah. All that talk about you loving Christmas turns me on. And I thought you deserved it with the day you had, so *A Christmas Story* it is." He smiles, grabbing our tickets from the attendant, then latching his hand back with mine before pulling me into the historical Bedford Cinema.

Ram got everything we ever possibly needed to watch a movie. Popcorn, soda, candy, a Slurpee, nachos, and a pretzel. Although I begged him not to waste all that money, he insisted, and before I knew it, we were seated in the back with two laps full of movie theater goodies.

The movie began and the moment the movie filled

the screen I was engrossed. I simply love Christmas. I sadly admit that every year I stalk all channels in hopes to find that one special channel that plays *A Christmas Story* over and over. I would have loved to see it in the theaters, but no one ever wanted to come with me. Every once in a while I turn to Ram, who is smiling, watching me. Here and there, our fingers graze as we both dig for a handful of popcorn. Me, trying to be polite, I always pull my hand away so he can get his scoop. He, on the other hand, always takes his handful and starts feeding me his scoop. It's just the sweetest, yet simplest thing anyone has ever done for me.

At the part where the dog eats the turkey, Ram slips his hand under the armrest, placing his palm on my hip. His skin on mine is like an inferno. I feel the heat of him instantly, causing me to take a hefty sip of my Slurpee to help bring my temperature down. I turn to him, curious about what he's up to, and he smiles. "This is the best part. Pay attention."

My cheeks flush at his words. Because they are filled with intent. He's up to something. I turn to the screen just as his hand moves closer and cups my sex over my leggings. A small gasp escapes my lips at his bold move. I look around the theater making sure no one is paying attention, which they aren't.

I'm trying to pretend I'm watching the movie, but over my leggings, he begins stroking my sex. Finding my secret spot and teasing me, he moves his hand higher, causing the armrest to raise. I slightly panic, afraid someone will see what he is doing, but he leans over and says, "Don't you just love it when the family comes together?

So satisfying." I moan softly, trying to pay attention to the movie. They did come together, finding themselves at a Chinese restaurant at Christmas. My favorite part is when they sing Christmas carols and laugh. Just as they begin to do that, Ram finds the elastic band at the top of my leggings and dips his hand inside, reaching past my saturated panties and into my sex. I moan louder than anticipated, and Ram chuckles next to me. I'm so embarrassed at what's happening. So afraid someone is watching, but so hot, and aroused. His finger pulls out and dips back into my hot sex, over and over again, in rhythm with the singing on the screen. I'm silently panting, and I find myself cupping his hand for more pressure. Just as they cut into the duck, I explode, coming all over his hand.

"You know you've ruined that movie for me now," I say, my cheeks still flushed from my orgasm.

He flashes me a wide grin. "Well, you made it for me. It will forever be my favorite movie, no matter the season."

We're walking back to his car, the silence falling over us. I don't want our night to end and I can tell he doesn't either. Being with Ram has been more than I could have ever expected. Actually, it's better. He's perfect in so many ways, and to know that he's real, and not hiding behind fake messages or lies, causes a flutter of happiness to explode inside me. Ram is the kind of man I have always dreamed about. Kind. Funny. Loyal. Super good looking. A gentleman, yet this beast of a man who takes me to levels I would otherwise be too shy to pursue. The realization hits me in waves. I no longer have any reservations about

Ram. And I want him to know that.

"Would you like to come back to my place?" I ask, hoping he doesn't notice the nervousness in my voice.

I watch his eyes darken and I'm worried I may have read his signals wrong. I open my mouth to apologize for getting the wrong impression when he speaks. "Buttercup, I thought you'd never ask. Get in the car. I plan on driving really fast."

And he does. I give him my address and with his muscle car weaving through traffic, before I know it, I'm unlocking the door to my apartment. With a shaky hand, I undo the lock and we both enter my tiny apartment. As I flick on the lights, Ram is picking me up, pressing my back to the wall.

"I feel like we've gotten to know each other pretty well, do you agree?" he asks, his warm breath smelling like nacho cheese. Some would find it gross, but I find it lovely. He bends down, gently pressing a soft kiss to the corner of my mouth.

"I would say so," I breathe, my words husky. He approves of my answer, dropping another kiss to my mouth.

"So then you would agree that you find me completely irresistible?" At that I laugh, watching his lips curl into a mischievous smile.

"Full of yourself much?" I smirk, watching his eyes light up.

"Yes, I am full of want for you." He brings his mouth to mine again, this time kissing me with intent. I wrap my arms around his neck, bringing our bodies smashing together. "You're perfect, you know that, right?" He nips at my bottom lip, sucking me into his mouth. His words ignite something inside me, as everything he says does, and I put more pressure into our kiss. My lips parting, and our tongues dancing around one another.

"I think you're quite fantastic, yourself." I thread my fingers into his hair, tugging at his thick mane. The growl that leaves his throat gives me the courage to tell him what I've been dreaming about doing since our first phone call. "I want you, Ram." His body stiffens, his mouth leaving mine. His eyes are intense, a fireball of emotions.

"Say that again," he demands, his voice deep with lust.

"I want you. I trust you. And I think we should take this relationship to the next level." He crashes his lips back on mine and our kiss becomes feral. I feel his hardness against my covered leggings, and the buildup of what I hope is to come excites me.

He pulls us away from the wall, walking us down my short hallway. "Second door," I breathe between kisses, and he enters my small bedroom.

Not needing any more direction, he walks over to my bed, and with me still cradled in his arms, crawls onto the bed, laying me back on the soft mattress. His body blankets mine as he spreads kisses down my throat to my neckline, pulling my thick sweater down to meet the bare skin of my collarbone. "You have the softest skin." He kisses along my shoulder. "God, there's this possessive side of me that wants to mark you everywhere so people will know you're mine." His teeth graze my shoulder blade, sending a heated wave of spasms to my core. "I need to see all of you," he says, leaning up and pushing my sweater up my waist. Our visual connection never falters as he lifts my sweater up and over my head. My tank top, along with my simple lavender bra, are next.

The growl erupting from his chest is enthralling as he takes in my exposed chest. The old part of me would try and cover myself, shy to be so exposed, but with Ram, I feel alive. The way he looks at me. The desire I see pouring from his eyes. "Christ," he breathes, dropping his mouth to my small breast, taking it fully into his mouth. My head arches back, my eyes shutting. The feeling of his warm breath, hot mouth, his wet tongue sucking on my nipples is almost too much. I moan, wrapping my fingers into his hair.

"Oh yes," I breathe. This is nothing like how I imagined it would be. It is so much more. My body is beginning to shake, the need for more becoming unbearable. The pulse in my sex begging for him to be inside me. "I need more of you, Ram. I need you inside me." My brazen words shock me, but I don't think too much of it. He brings out this side I never knew existed. And ever since he fell into my life, he has woken this person inside me.

Releasing my right breast and working his magic on the other, he hums into my skin. "I've wanted you since day one. Ever since your dirty comment about how well you sucked cock." I smack him in his head, feeling the vibrations of his soft chuckle against my skin. He releases my nipple with a pop and sits forward, locking his vision with mine. "You could have told me you hated cock and I would still have found you perfect. I've wanted you for you." He leans forward, tapping gently on my head, and then on my heart. I fight to not start crying because it's been way too long that someone has appreciated me for me.

"I think we've done enough talking, Ram," I choke out, fighting my own emotions. He leans down, pressing his lips to mine before sitting back up.

"Are you sure about this?"

"Never been surer," I reply.

"You swear? Because once I get started with you, there is no stopping me."

I smile, hoping he keeps that vow. "Pinky promise."

"All right then, Buttercup, looks like it's go time."

The remainder of our clothes are discarded faster than humanly possible. My eyes grow large in size at his giant man part. As he rolls the condom down his long shaft he catches eyes with me and smirks. "You keep looking all hungry like that and I'm going to have to for real test out your cock sucking theory." My cheeks flare, not in embarrassment, but with the fact that I *want* to do that to him. And really badly, actually. Ram chuckles again. "We have all night, Buttercup."

I reach my hand out, stopping him from rolling the remainder of the condom on his dick. "Wait." He pauses, his eyes questioning. "Take it off. I want to feel you now." I watch his eyes light up. His hand grips his cock as it twitches at my request.

"You sure? You don't have—"

"Don't tell me what I have and don't have to do. I want your cock in my mouth. Now let me." *Who's this person who just said all that?* I think we both look shocked at my filthy mouth. But Ram quickly snaps out of it and jumps off me, lying next to me on the bed. Placing his hands behind his head, he watches as I sit up and position myself down the bed and over his engorged cock.

"You can stop when you want, you don't have to—"

I shut him up when I bring my lips to the top of his impressive length, my tongue licking the salty bead of pre-cum on his tip. Finding my boldness, I wrap my tiny hands around his shaft and put him fully into my mouth. My jaw aches, almost painfully, at stretching my mouth so wide around his girth. Daryl's dick was nothing in comparison to Ram's. This one is powerful and thick and delicious and mine.

His moan is instant as he spears his long fingers into my hair. It gives me the courage to pull out and bring my mouth back down, this time taking him deeper. "Fuck Dani, this feels amazing." I take my praise and work his shaft faster, bobbing up and down. His dick is large, so it's hard to fit him fully in my mouth. When I take my free hand and gently massage his balls, his restraint snaps and he takes control of my movements, lifting his hips, working himself harder and faster in my mouth. "Fuck, you're so sweet… fuck…" he grunts with each thrust. I'm trying to relax my jaw but gag a few times. He tries to let up but I push on him, fighting the restriction.

"Baby, I'm gonna come, fuck… I'm going to…"

I take him deeper, letting him know I want him to come in my mouth. This is something new to me, and I'm unsure what to expect. Ram grunts, the feel of him getting thicker—if possible—is followed by the release of his seed down my throat.

Before I'm able to suck him completely dry, he's pulling me off him, flipping me on the bed. "Your turn." His smile is simply devilish. He doesn't allow me any time to comprehend his next move, and before I know it, his tongue is licking at my center.

"Oh my God," I moan, the feeling of his tongue is exhilarating on my pulsating lips. He takes no mercy on me as he laps up my juices, biting at my lips and working me in record speed to orgasm. Unable to control my body movements, I begin thrashing in his hold. His touch, his hot breath sucking me, it's all too much. "I can't…" I moan, needing him to stop, needing so much more.

"You can. Is this what it feels like to fuck you with three fingers, Buttercup?" And with that, he pushes three thick fingers into me. I explode, white lights exploding behind my eyelids. My throat locks, unable to scream.

Working me through my spasms, my legs finally unclench, releasing the strangling hold I have on his head. He crawls up my body, covering me with his strong form. He rolls a new condom down his length, giving me a mischievous look, like he's wondering if I'll stop him this time. I smile back, taking a peek at his thick cock, and lick my lips. Pushing my legs apart with his knees, Ram places himself at the center of my sex. "Ready?" he asks, his voice thick.

"Set, go," I reply. And with that quirky smile I love so much, he thrusts into me.

There is no way to explain the feeling of him being so deep inside me. He pulls out slowly, then works himself back inside. My juices are coating his thick length, making it slick for him as he pumps in and out of me.

"I forgot to add one more thing to my favorite things list," he pants, pulling out before slamming back home. "You. I like you." He drops his mouth to mine, kissing me with a ferocity unlike any other time we've kissed.

Our bodies are slamming into one another, a slick layer of sweat building. "This… This is almost as wonderful as Christmas carols and cheese," I moan, just as his hand squeezes my nipple. I feel his chuckle in my mouth and my lips curl into a smile. It doesn't stop him from ravaging my mouth. All while working my body into a frenzied mess.

"'Tis the season to fuck the most beautiful woman, fra, ra ra ra *rahhhh…*" he trails off as my hands grab his butt cheeks and I squeeze my nails, possibly breaking skin. Playtime is suddenly over and Ram takes control. Or loses it. He starts pounding into me as if he needs to get deeper, farther inside me. I'm a wild mess scraping, pulling, and grabbing all of him, until his grunted hiss matches my heavy moan as we both come.

Chapter Ten

Ram

> **Are Your Parents Siblings?**

"**Y**OU GOT 'RAMMED,'" I TELL HER, A SMUG GRIN painting my face as I clean her with a warm rag.

"Oh my God," she groans. "Your corny jokes are worse than mine!"

I laugh as I climb off the bed and start dressing. It's been a week since we ran into each other at her ex's office and we've been attached at the hip ever since. Each day, I pick her up at her place after work. We go have dinner or do something fun. And then we end up in her bed, where I make her scream my name until she's hoarse. She's yet to ask me to stay over, but I don't even care. Because by morning, she texts me right when she wakes and it turns into a full day of sexual banter.

"You better hurry and get dressed," I tell her as I drop

the used condom into the trash and pull on a pair of black boxer briefs.

She's still sprawled out on the bed, her pale skin slightly reddened everywhere I kissed her from the stubble on my face. Her dark hair is in a wild mess on the pillow and her pouty lip is jutted out. My dick responds to her sexy little mouth.

"Keep looking at me like that with your gorgeous lips looking wet and tempting, and we'll never make it to the restaurant in time," I tell her with a wicked grin. "Besides, we need to celebrate. That idiot finally gave you your money back and you are free."

At this, she smiles. "He looked scared. And his stupid neighbor girlfriend wisely sat in the car."

I pull on my jeans and toss her the black inside-out leggings she was wearing earlier. "Well, you were holding a container of bologna like it was a bomb about to detonate. I'm not sure he knew what you planned to do with it, but he wasn't taking any chances."

Her giggles warm me as she slides out of the bed. I crave to bite her cute little ass but before I have a chance, she's slipping on a pair of pink lacy panties. "I gave him the stink-eye, huh? He was scared of me," she tells me in a smug voice.

I toss her sweater at her and then look for my black thermal shirt. By the time I'm fully dressed, she's nearly clothed as well.

"I'm sorry but why you ever dated that washed up loser is beyond me. It was like you had an uncle fetish and you settled on him to fulfill said fetish," I tell her, wagging my eyebrows.

"Gross," she says and pretends to gag. "He does kind of look like someone's uncle, though."

After we're both dressed, I snag her wrist and pull her to me. The air still smells like sex, and I fucking love it. I've never been so damned happy in all my life. Back when I dated Chelsea, I thought I was happy. Little did I realize, I wasn't even close.

With Dani, I smile non-stop. She makes me laugh and appreciate the smallest things, like her tiny sighs and whispered apologies. I like listening to her throaty voice chatting about her day after I've made love to her. I like how her fingernails—now a nude polish but still chipped—run through my hair as she scratches my scalp when we're just lying in bed together. She soothes parts of me I didn't know were upset. Her presence warms parts of me that I didn't realize where cold and bitter.

We're all flirting and laughter as we drive to the restaurant where we're meeting Roman and Andie. Dani thought it would be fun for us all to get together. But as soon as we trot up to the restaurant with Dani tucked against my side and under my arm, I can't help but wonder if it was a bad idea.

Roman is scowling with his arms crossed.

Andie glares at him as if he shit in her food.

I mean, the first and only time they "met" was when Roman knocked Dani down while he was shitfaced. I can see why there might be bad blood between them.

"Why the long faces?" Dani questions, her voice strained.

Roman lets out a growl. "Your friend thinks it's funny to kick people she doesn't like."

Andie scoffs and flips him off. "You were on your phone. Not paying attention. And wham!" She claps her leather-gloved hands together for effect. "Slammed right into me. Now my ass is wet from falling in the snow!"

He glowers at her. "And when I offered my hand to help you back up," he snaps through clenched teeth, "you fucking kicked me. Again."

Andie smirks and shrugs. "You deserved it. Payback from last time."

"But you also kicked me last time. When does it end, woman?" he roars.

Dani tenses in my arms. Things are escalating quickly. I need to get them to chill the fuck out. "All right, you two. Into the restaurant. Both of you need a drink. We can all be friends here. No phones," I order to my brother. Then I make eye contact with Andie. "And no kicking. Let's be friends."

They both huff and stomp into the restaurant.

Dani looks up at me with a frown on her face. "Gah, I don't like that they hate each other."

My brows furrow and I dust some falling snow off her cheek. "It's just one dinner. If they get too bad, I'll send Roman home."

She seems satisfied with my answer and we head inside, hand in hand. The restaurant is also a bar. It's swanky and dark. The lights are low and candles are on each table. With the dark mahogany of the furniture, it's easy to feel like you're in some cave or something. We settle into the booth where Andie and Roman are sitting an exaggerated distance apart on the same side. Dani and I slide in across from them, and she practically sits in my lap with her leg draped over my thigh.

"You guys look so happy," Andie says in a sugary sweet voice. "Dani did well. You're a thoughtful gentleman." Her eyes cut over to my brother. "Unlike some assholes around here."

Roman growls, but she isn't awarded his answer because a waitress shows up.

"What can I get you all?" she questions, chomping noisily on her gum.

Dani pipes up. "Shots of tequila all around. This group needs it. Then bring two vodka tonics for the ladies." Andie raises her eyebrows in surprise at Dani ordering for them. I squeeze Dani's leg supportively because she looks so cute when she gets all confident and takes charge.

"I'll take a Jack and Coke," I tell the server.

"Same," Roman grumbles. "Make mine a double."

The woman bounces off and Andie rolls her eyes. "Here we go."

Before they have another shouting match, I shove menus in front of them. "Find something to eat, and for the love of God, don't talk to each other."

Dani laughs and thus begins our night.

Two hours later, a belly full of food, and more alcohol than four adults should consume, things are much lighter. Instead of being hateful, Andie and Roman have taken to slinging hilarious insults at each other that have the four of us laughing. It's progress.

"Don't you love nature?" Andie asks, faux curiosity on her face. She even fingers a blonde strand of hair innocently. Roman fucking falls for it because his hard gaze softens. "Despite what it did to you," she finishes with a giggle.

He rolls his eyes while Dani and I crack up.

"I wasn't born with enough middle fingers to let you know how I feel about you," he says sadly. "So it's just Fuck and You." He waggles his middle fingers and his grin is wicked.

"Burn," Dani snorts, and slings back another shot.

I smirk at her and squeeze her thigh again. It feels good to be having fun.

"You're the only reason the gene pool needs a life-guard," Andie tells him, her lips curving up in a smile.

Roman cracks a smile but tries to hide it. "I love what you've done with your hair," he says in a genuine tone. Her lips part just a bit but then he continues, "How do you get it to come out of your nostrils like that?"

"Asshole!" Andie barks and swats at him. Her cheeks turn slightly pink and I can tell it embarrassed her.

"I'm sorry," Roman teases and hauls her to him. "Give big daddy a hug."

She squirms and squeals as he gives her an over-the-top bear hug. He lets go with a grunt.

"You punched my nuts," he chokes out in surprise.

Dani is giggling so hard I think she's going to hyper-ventilate. "You gotta watch your nuts around Andie. She's like a squirrel. No nut is safe." This time it's Dani who gets kicked by Andie.

"Ow!"

"How many times do I have to flush before you go away?" Andie says to him.

Roman snorts, which makes Andie start to giggle. I don't miss the fact that she hasn't moved back to her side of the booth. They're still close. Within kicking and nut-punching distance. My brother is brave, especially because of the way he keeps slinging stupid insults at her.

"Hell is wallpapered with all your deleted selfies," he says with a laugh.

"I was going to give you a nasty look, but you already have one," she retorts.

His eyes narrow. "You're not as bad as people say. You're much, much worse."

"Just because you have one doesn't mean you have to act like one." Andie smirks and then mouths the word "dick."

My brother shrugs his shoulders. "You have the right to remain silent because whatever you say will probably be stupid anyway."

"Your cock is so small, you could use it to floss teeth," she snarls.

He laughs. "Are your parents siblings?"

"I'm blonde," she clips out, a grin on her lips. "What's your excuse?"

"Jesus loves you," he sighs, "but everyone else thinks you're an asshole."

"You're street smart. *Sesame Street* smart." She pretends to dust her nails off on the front of her shirt.

"Okay, you two," I say with a chuckle. "We've paid the bill and people are waiting to sit here. Besides…" I trail off, pointing between them both. "I have just the way to finish this war."

Ten minutes later, we're on the side of the building standing in the snow under the moonlight. Dani is drunk as a skunk and leans against me, her giggles making the night sound musical.

"The rules are," I tell them as I bend and pack some snow into my palm. "There are no rules."

I launch the snowball at Andie, but Roman blocks it with his chest. Both girls scream and, next thing I know, snow is flying from every direction. I end up taking one to the face and it blinds me for a second. Then, I feel ice go down the crack of my ass. Dani's giggles give her away and the moment my eyes clear, I charge after her. She makes a weak attempt to throw snow at me, but I'm quicker. I tackle her into the snow. Of course, the thick blanket of it softens her fall. But nothing softens my dick. I'm hard as ice pressed up against her soft body.

The snow starts falling harder. I can hear Roman and Andie hollering at each other behind me, but right now it's just Dani and I. Her hazel eyes are hooded and she gives me that *kiss me* stare I love so much. Snowflakes dust her forehead and cheeks. I decide she's never looked more beautiful.

"You make me happy," I tell her, my voice low.

Her legs slip out from under me and she hooks them at my waist. I press my length against her as my lips hover over hers.

"You make me happy too, Ram." Her eyes twinkle with delight. It does fucking fabulous things to my heart.

Our lips meet and I kiss her softly at first. The snow is cold but our bodies are heated. I grind against her as we kiss, drinking down every single moan that escapes her. By the time we no longer hear Andie and Roman, I've worked Dani into quite a state. Her eyes are closed and her head is tilted back in ecstasy.

"I'm obsessed with you," I admit with a growl and tug at her bottom lip with my teeth. "So fucking obsessed."

She whimpers and her teeth start to chatter.

"Shit," I groan. "I need to get you out of this snow and someplace warm."

I scoop her from the snow and stride toward the parking lot. My car is blanketed in new snow. Between the weather and my drinking, we're going to have to get an Uber for the ride home. When we reach my car, I turn on the ignition to heat it up.

"I need to get you out of these wet clothes," I tell her, concern painting my voice.

She doesn't argue when I begin undressing her in the parking lot. We're in a darkened corner and she's too liquored up to care about bystanders. Once I have her down to her bra and panties and she's shivering, I pull off my thermal and dress her in it. Then, I open the back seat. Once we're settled into the quickly warming car and our wet clothes are shoved to the floorboard, I pull her into my lap. My cock strains through my jeans, but I'm content with just warming her up right now.

My palms caress her flesh under the shirt while she hugs my neck. Her tits, hidden by the thin fabric of my shirt and her bra, are in my face and she smells so goddamned good. Like vodka and the fried pickles from earlier. I never thought those two scents would make my mouth water.

"I need you," she whines, her hips swaying in a sexy-as-fuck way. "Now." She peels away my shirt and tosses it onto the floor.

I tear at her bra until it gets thrown far from her

supple tits. My palms grip her ass as I haul her to me. I bite at her nipple, each time harder than before, until she's begging me to stop.

"Say the magic word," I tease, tonguing her sensitive flesh.

"Please."

"No."

"What?"

I grin up at her. "The magic word is *no*. Remember? You're still learning that one. Tell me no and I'll stop."

Her hair is wet and drips water onto her fine tits. When she bites on her bottom lip in a contemplative way, I nearly come in my pants. She looks so fucking hot.

"No," she murmurs. "Okay, let's try it again."

Chuckling, I lean forward and start sucking on her nipple.

"Mmmm…"

I bite gently.

"Yesssss," she hisses out.

Until I bite her again.

"Holy crap, Ram!"

"Magic word," I taunt.

I bite her again and she slaps me. "You're going to leave bruises."

"I'll stop when you tell me no," I remind her. This time, I bite her hard enough to make her squeal.

"You…You…" she snarls, her fingers gripping my hair. "Punk."

I start rubbing her over her clit through her panties until she starts whimpering. Then, I bite her again.

"Ow!"

"Say the word, Buttercup," I growl, my teeth raking over her tender flesh. "Say it."

"No," she huffs.

"Was that so bad?"

She glares down at me, but there's heat in her eyes. "I said no, I won't say it. Not no to what you're doing."

I raise an eyebrow up at her. "You like it when I bite you, baby?" My finger circles her clit again.

"I do," she murmurs and juts her sexy tit back in my face.

"Then by all means," I tease as I rake my teeth over her pebbled nipple. "Let me serve her royal highness."

She moans when I tongue her nipple. "That's more like it, servant boy."

At that, I bite her nipple. It earns me a slap to the head again, but she's riding my finger even harder than before.

"If you like it when I bite you here," I breathe against her sweet nipple. I pinch her clit through the lace. "Then you're going to love it when I bite you here."

She shudders in my arms and I keep the pressure on her clit. I nip and suck at her breasts until she's pushing me away. With us both being drunk, it takes a moment to get fully naked and situated. Then, I have her beneath me. My dick slides against her pussy, eager to be inside her.

Everything is hazy but when I stare into her hooded eyes, it all becomes clear. She's my focus. I'm fucking obsessed with her, just like I told her.

"Tell me no," I murmur, my lips just brushing against hers as I tease her cunt with the tip of my cock.

"Yessss," she pleads. Her heels dig into my ass and she pushes me into her hot, receptive body. We both hiss in pleasure. "Don't stop, Ram. Don't ever stop."

I start thrusting into her fast and hard. "I don't plan on it, baby."

When she cries out again and her pussy clenches around my dick, I lose control. My heat rushes from me and I mark my woman. I've left bite marks all over her body. Now I leave a trail of my semen marking her from the inside too.

Our eyes lock and something changes in our heated gazes. The air feels thicker. We feel more real.

"I like you, Buttercup," I breathe against her parted lips.

Her palm strokes my cheek and she smiles. "I like you too."

Problem is…I lied.

Like isn't a strong enough word to describe how I feel about her. I'm falling hard for his adorable woman. I just hope she falls too.

Chapter Eleven

Dani

Two Truths and a Lie

"OH, WHY THANK YOU, MR. SORENSON, BUT I'M sure the missus would miss you greatly if we ran off together." I smile, handing him his deposit slip. I swear, one of these days his wife is going to come storming through those bank doors with a broom ready to beat me.

The doors whip open and I see Andie, looking disheveled, race into the bank. I open my mouth to ask what happened to her, but she puts her hand up. "Don't ask." And with that, she walks behind the teller booths, shoving her jacket underneath.

"I wasn't going to. But you have some—" She swats my hand away as I attempt to pull some fern out of her hair. "What happ—"

"Zip it." She raises her fingers to make a motion of

sealing her mouth before turning back to her register. What's gotten into her?

"I was just going to—"

"I got mauled by a wild dog. Damn thing attacked me," she bites out, punching in her code to clock in.

"Oh my goodness. Are you okay?" I ask, checking for any bites or bleeding.

"Oh, *I'm fine*. He's not, though. Thinking he can just catch me off guard and tackle me."

I'm staring at her, confused. Why would a dog just jump on her? I think about how she acted strange over the weekend. Anytime I called, she'd been quick to get off the phone. One time telling me she was working out, and then with her heavy breathing, she hung up on me.

"Okaaay." I shrug my shoulders and help the next customer. The morning rush finally dies down and I'm dying to text Ram. I made him some homemade cookies to bring to work, because I know he was up late working on some sort of client portfolio.

"Oh my God, these cookies are to die for." I turn to see Andie all up in my goods. "Hey!" I snatch the half eaten cookie from her hand. "Those aren't for you!"

Trying to take back her cookie, she huffs. "Why not? They were in your locker."

"Yeah," I grumble. "Because I was going to bring them to Ram at work on my lunch."

"But what about me? I need love and cookies too," she pouts, putting her hands out as she waits for me to give in, which I do. She then shoves another cookie in her mouth. "Aww thanks, I knew you loved me. Speaking of love, how is lover boy?"

I smile anytime I think of Ram. About our relationship. I swore he was going to tell me he loved me in the back of his car. And for some crazy reason, I could have said it back. He makes me feel happy. Whole. Like I can do anything as long as I have him by my side. And I can't say that I have felt that with anyone.

"You two finish up what you perverts started in the snow on Friday night?" she asks, trying to get the last bite of her cookie down. I blush at the memory of our car sex. How the snow covered the windows, blanketing us in. How he took me twice in his car, with no care who could possibly see.

"Yeah, I guess you can say that. And what happened to you and Roman? You two seemed to also disappear." All of a sudden, Andie chokes on whatever remaining cookie's still in her mouth.

"Oh no! Are you *okay*?" I pat her back, handing her my water bottle.

"Shit, I'm fine."

"So…what happened to you two?"

"Nothing. Why? What do you think happened to us?"

I give her a quizzical stare. "I'm not sure, hence why I'm asking. Is there something I should know that happened?" Ram and I were so lost in our own moment, we never said goodbye to them. Andie's behavior, though, sure is piquing my curiosity.

"Ew! Don't even," she huffs. "I wouldn't touch that douche with a ten-foot pole."

"Sure you wouldn't." I begin to chuckle.

"I wouldn't! I hate that guy. He's like the scum on my shoe that steps in dog shit then more dog shit. He's dog shit scum."

For someone who doesn't like said person, she sure is working hard to prove just how much she doesn't like him. I drop it and text Ram, letting him know about my new findings.

> Me: Do you know if anything is going on between Andie and Roman? Andie is acting weird.
> Ram: Not that I know of...besides that he doesn't think too highly of her. No offense. I know she's your best friend but he's definitely not into her.
> Me: None taken. The feeling is mutual. I think. Did Roman ever come home Friday night?
> Ram: Babe, I was balls deep in you all night, then came home and crashed thinking about how good you feel around me. The last thing I was doing was wondering if Roman made curfew.

I laugh at his crude wording. At one point in my life, I would have blushed or been too embarrassed to associate with such words, but Ram has this way of turning these hot shameful words into sexual triggers for me. I smile, typing off a new message.

> Me: You're right. And I'm still sorry for smashing the snowball in your face while waiting for our Uber. I just couldn't resist.
> Ram: And I'm sorry for retaliating. Your cheeks were just so flushed still from my cock after I fucked you that you looked

like you needed to cool off.

And just like that, he has my cheeks flaring, remembering his cock, the way I rode him. My smile is evident.

Me: Well I want to make it up to you. I made you my special cookies. I can come by your office on my lunch.

I wait for his normal quick response, but this time I don't get any. I watch the three dots light up and then disappear. I wouldn't think it strange if it wasn't the third time in the past week he's done this. Every time I offer to meet him at his office, he blows me off. Going from matching me text for text to nothing. Then messaging me an hour later, claiming he got caught up with work and he would see me when he picked me up.

I try and think back on every time we discussed his job and realize he was always so vague, changing the subject, or turning the conversation on me. The realization rattles me that he might be hiding something from me. Far from the timid girl before, I type out a message.

Me: Fine, you must be busy. Again. No need to pick me up later. I don't want to take up any more of your time at work.

I huff, tossing my phone next to my drawer, but it dings almost immediately.

Ram: I'm sorry. Don't be mad. I just have some things I'm working out. It's not a good time around here.

Great, so now he's keeping things from me. I was getting the feeling that we were very honest and open with one another. If he had something going on at work but didn't feel he could talk to me, that hurt even more.

Me: Then talk to me. What's wrong? Do you not want me to come to your work? Are you embarrassed of me?

This time he doesn't text back. He calls. I step away from my window to take his call.

"Don't ever say that," he growls. "I could never be embarrassed of you. You're perfect and amazing. And if anything, it would be the other way around."

"Then what's wrong? Do you not trust me to tell me what's wrong so I could help?"

"Buttercup, it's not that. I promise. You're the one person I do trust. Listen. I'm coming to get you. Tell Sphincter you're sick. I need to be with you. I don't like you sounding unsure of us."

I sigh into the phone, feeling exactly what he said. Unsure. I feel bad it took something so small for me to quickly doubt him. "I'm sorry Ram—"

"Do *not* apologize to me. I lo—I'm just coming to get you." The phone goes dead.

I tell Harold that I have a bad case of diarrhea because Andie says that works all the time. He purses his thin lips at me, telling me he needs to know no more and to go home. Ram is there by the time I've gathered my things, and I exit the bank.

Always so handsome, he is leaning against his Mustang, his hands covered in his leather jacket pocket. I walk up to him shyly, embarrassed about how I acted. "You really should invest in a winter jacket. Cool leather jackets don't keep a common cold or flu away," I say as he grabs for the lapels of my coat, bringing me to him. He kisses me, knowing exactly what I need, and doesn't stop until both of us are in need of air.

"I don't need a warmer jacket. You keep me hot enough."

I smile, smacking him in his chest as he walks me to the passenger side door and helps me into his car. Getting in himself, he takes off, his wheels spinning in the snow. The ride home is quiet. As much as I know he's not mad at me, I still feel the tension.

"Will you tell me what's bothering you at work?" Stupid me. I ask the one question I can tell he doesn't want to answer. His hands grab the steering wheel tighter, and I notice the small twitch in his jaw.

"Dani, I told you it was nothing. Just let it go," he snaps. But then his tone softens. "Please." He turns back to the road, leaving us in silence for the rest of the drive to his place. He just called me Dani. My heart hurts at the way he just spoke to me.

"Fuck, I'm sorry." He pulls over on the side of the road. I'm uneasy, knowing it's not safe with the weather, and cars sliding from the snowy conditions.

"Ram, just keep driving. It's not safe."

"Yeah, well I can't knowing that you're pissed at me." I can tell he's frustrated, but right now, so am I.

"Well, maybe if you weren't being so secretive, I wouldn't be worried you were lying to me. Daryl lied—"

He slams his fists onto the steering wheel startling me. "Do not compare me to Daryl. I am nothing like him."

"If you're lying to me," I tell him in a wobbly voice, "then you are."

He doesn't say anything more. A short time of silence passes before he turns, bringing us back onto the road.

We make it safely back to his place with no more conversation. He parks and helps me out of the car so I don't slip. Instead of grabbing my hand and walking me to his apartment door, he holds me. I want to stand my ground and push him away, but his touch is comforting and I can't say no to him.

"Listen. I'm sorry. I'm so sorry. I'll explain everything, okay? Just let me get you inside and get you warm and something to eat. Then we can talk, all right?"

I nod, knowing that he's trying. He presses a soft kiss to my lips, and then takes my hand to escort me inside.

Once the door shuts and we're inside his apartment, we both brush off the snow that picked up quickly from our short walk. "Here, let me take your coat—"

Just then, the door opens behind me and Roman hurries inside.

"Oh, shit. Um, hey. I didn't think anyone would be here," he rambles.

"Why? I live here, asshole," Ram says to his brother. "Why are *you* here?"

Roman grunts. "I had to pick up some things."

Ram is looking at his brother peculiarly. "Dude, is your shirt ripped? Is that a *hickey*?" We both lean in and Roman bounces back.

"No, why would I have a hickey?" Guilt drips from his comment. "Enough about me, why are *you* here? Don't you have interviews?"

Ram stiffens beside me, staring hard at Roman.

"What, did something go wrong with the Inigo job? Shit, I thought you locked that one in."

"Shut up, Roman."

"What? It's okay if it fell through. More jobs will come along."

"Roman, just drop it—"

I look to Ram, then back at Roman.

"Wait, what job? I thought you worked for some big firm as a marketing executive or manager or something?"

"You mean *I* work for Tucker Advertising. That's *my* job," Roman clarifies.

I stare at Roman, confused. I look back and forth between Roman who looks clueless and Ram who looks about ready to murder his brother.

Then it hits me.

He *has* been lying to me.

Turning to Ram, I huff. "You *don't* work for a company, do you?"

Roman swears under his breath, putting his shoes back on and mumbling something about needing to run an errand he forgot about. As the door shuts, Ram slowly brings his eyes to mine. I don't want to show emotion, but it's too hard. It's built in me.

"You lied to me," I say softly. Feeling the hurt deep inside. Ram takes a step toward me, but I put my hand up to stop him.

"What else have you been lying to me about?" I ask. I stare him down, demanding the truth. I won't take any more lies. From anyone.

"Only my job."

"Why?"

"Because I didn't want you to think I was a loser. How was I supposed to know we would end up here?"

"Where? In a safe place with one another? A place

where I trusted you? I told you everything about me."

I can tell he's back on the defensive. "You weren't honest with me at first either. *Carrie? Bartender?* At least I told you my real name."

What a low blow. "Yeah, because I didn't know you. I was protecting myself."

He comes at me this time, ignoring my plea to stay away. He brings his arms around me pulling our bodies together.

"I would never hurt you, Buttercup. I promise you. I lied, yes. But it was because I was fucking embarrassed. What if you didn't like me because I was jobless?"

I look into his eyes that are begging for me to understand. And I do understand. I would have never changed how I felt, or how my feelings grew like wildfire for him over the past month, job or not.

I raise my hands cupping his cheeks. "Ram, I would have never judged you for not having a job. Haven't I shown you that that's not what's important to me?"

"You have, baby, and I'm sorry I lied. Don't fucking leave me. Please." His words gut me. The pain of even thinking to leave him hurts almost as much as actually walking out that door. I bring his mouth to mine, pressing my lips to his.

"I'm not. But don't lie to me, Ram. Please. It will be a deal breaker for me. Okay?"

"Deal. I never will." He kisses me back until we're both winded.

"I have to ask," I murmur as I pull away. "So you don't work for a corporate company and dress in a suit all day?"

"I used to. I lied about working there but, truth is, I

did at one point. Not anymore."

I take in his statement. "Okay, so what did Roman mean about a client calling you back?"

"I'm trying to go solo. Build up my own client base. I build websites and do branding for companies. If I can get a solid list of clients, then I can build the groundwork for a pretty badass marketing business."

I don't know why he doesn't see how wonderful he truly is. I kiss him again, and this time he lifts me, kicking off my wet boots and then he carries me over to the couch. He sits down with me straddling his lap.

"I want to play a game with you, okay?"

I nod, because I love his games. They always end up with me in some crazy position, begging for more of him.

"It's called two truths and a lie. Have you heard of it?"

I giggle because I have. Andie and I used to play it in elementary school.

He kisses my lips quickly, making sure our eyes are locked. "One lie. My job. I may not have one now, but I'm working on it and hopefully I'll be doing something that makes you proud of me."

I bring my hands up cupping his face. "Ram, I *am* proud of you."

Another quick peck. "Now for one truth. Ever since I met you, I've never felt so alive. So eager to make something of myself. To be better. To be somebody you want to keep in your life for a very long time." His confession hits me like a tidal wave, my heart cracking open letting him in. Fully in.

"Oh Ram, I feel the same way," I murmur as I lean in to kiss him. Our silent vows confessing through our lips,

136

our connection. He eventually pulls away, both our eyes glazed with emotion.

"Babe, there's one more truth."

"Okay," I say with a nod, needing him to spit it out so he can carry me to his room and make me his.

"I love you."

Chapter Twelve

Ram

> ## Your Mom Is so Dumb.

TOLD HER I LOVED HER. YESTERDAY, AFTER OUR FIRST official "fight" as a couple, I professed my love. And what did she say back?

Thank you.

I was so stunned by her not returning the sentiment that I had to distract myself with kissing her so that I wouldn't sit there staring stupidly at her. Our kiss led to petting. Petting led to tearing off clothes. Tearing off clothes led to hot sex for the rest of the day. Neither she nor I brought it up again.

Now, here it is over twenty-four hours later, and I'm still fucked in the head over her words.

Thank you.

God, I feel like such an idiot.

"If you don't stir that sauce, it's going to burn," Roman

chides from behind me.

I snap out of my daze and stir the spaghetti sauce, but not before giving him an annoyed grunt.

He walks over to me and leans his hip on the counter beside me. His massive arms are crossed over his chest as he scrutinizes me. "What's got you so distracted, man?"

I turn the sauce on low heat and cover it with a lid before answering him. "It's Dani."

"I thought you two made up. Aren't her and her psycho friend coming over for dinner soon?" he questions, his dark brows furled together in question.

"Yeah," I say with a huff. "It's just that I told her I loved her and she didn't say it back."

I feel like a pussy even saying the words.

Roman lets out a chuckle. "She loves you."

Snapping my head to look at him, I scowl. "But how do *you* know this?"

He shrugs his shoulders and tugs at the top button of his crisp white dress shirt. After coming home from work, he shed his jacket and tie but is still the ever-perfect Roman. "I know this, little brother," he says with a grin, "because of the way she looks at you. Every time she sees you, her eyes light up. Every time you give her the D, her moans wake me up. She laughs at all of your stupid jokes and always seems to need to be touching you in some way. Her smile is always on whenever you're around. She loves you, man. Trust me."

My heart tightens at his words. "So why didn't she say it back?"

His expression becomes thoughtful. "I don't know. Maybe she was mad at you for lying. Or perhaps she was just scared. Give the poor girl some time. You're kind of overbearing at times. Most women would call you a stalker. Apparently Dani likes your stalker ass." Then he chuckles. "Excuse me…*loves*. Just give her time to admit that."

I let out a rush of breath. "Thanks. I thought you had a date, anyway. Don't you need to get out of here? You don't have to entertain Andie. I know you guys hate each other."

His easygoing expression hardens. Fire flickers in his eyes and his jaw clenches. Touchy subject?

"The date fell through. And this is my loft, too. I'm not leaving. I've had a helluva day today and am just hungry, for fuck's sake. Are you trying to get rid of me?" he snaps.

I playfully punch his brooding ass in the shoulder. "Lighten up, asshole. There's plenty of food, and you're always cool to eat whatever I make. I was just trying to save you from Andie. Why was your day bad? Those fuckers at Tucker giving you a hard time?"

He swallows and his throat bobs. "You could say that. Just biding my time."

His response makes me curious, but then the doorbell rings. Roman tears out of the kitchen to answer it. Soon, Dani and Andie come waltzing into the kitchen. Dani bounces over to me and throws her arms around my middle, kissing my back as I cook. I pat her hand and flash Andie a smile. But Andie isn't smiling back. She's glaring at Roman with narrowed eyes and pursed lips.

"I missed you," Dani tells me, the palms of her hands roaming my hardened abs through my T-shirt.

Chuckling, I turn my head so I can steal a kiss. "I missed you too, babe."

She pulls away and starts rummaging around the

cabinets for plates. Andie and Roman are still involved in a silent standoff. I notice Andie is dressed oddly similar to Roman. She wears a white silky button-up blouse tucked into a light grey skirt that flares out. Her black heels make her almost as tall as him. Both Roman and Andie have their arms crossed over their chests.

Awkward.

I don't know why he doesn't just leave now that she's here.

"Everything's ready," I tell them as I turn off the stove. My eyes roam over to Dani who looks sexy as hell tonight wearing another signature outfit of hers. Warm black sweater. Pale pink leggings. Black fuzzy boots. "Time to eat up, Buttercup," I tell her with a wink. Her cheeks blaze crimson and Andie groans from beside her.

"Let's eat before I lose my appetite," Andie mutters.

"Your mom is so dumb. She thinks menopause is a button on the DVD player," Andie tells Roman, her eyes narrowed.

I pour Dani another glass of wine. It's just getting good with Roman and Andie. Once they've drank a little, they're quite entertaining with their insults.

Roman scoffs and pushes his empty plate of spaghetti away. "Well, your mom is so dumb, that when the doctor asked her if she's sexually active, she said, 'no, I just lay there.'"

Andie rolls her eyes. "Is that all you got? Your mom is so dumb, she thought a runny nose was an exercise."

Roman laughs. "Your mom is so dumb, she thought

Starbucks was a bank."

She turns her chair to face him and leans forward, leveling a hard gaze at him. "Well, your mom is so dumb, first time she used a vibrator, she broke her two front teeth."

Roman pretends to gag. "Your mom is so dumb, she got fired from a blow job."

Dani sniggers and flashes me an amused look.

"Your mom is so dumb," Andie tells him, a wicked smile on her lips, "that she shoved cat food down her pants to feed her pussy."

Another faux gag from Roman. "Your mom is so dumb, she thought Taco Bell was a Mexican phone company."

Andie flips Roman off. "Your mom is so dumb, the smartest thing to come out of her mouth was a penis."

"Gross," he groans. "Your mom is so dumb, she thought asphalt was a butt disorder."

Andie lets out a giggle, which makes Roman beam in return. If they didn't hate each other so much, I'd say there was something sparking between those two.

"Your mom is so dumb," she tells him, "she thought *The Exorcist* was a workout video!"

Dani snorts wine through her nose and Andie high-fives her. I'm chuckling, and the worrying over Dani not telling me she loves me seems to be a thing of the past. Roman was right. She does love me. I can feel it by the way she grabs my hand and gives it a reassuring squeeze. Or the private smiles she sends me that promise so much once we close the bedroom door. I don't need the words right now because I have her.

"Come on," Dani says, "let's go start the movie while

these two knuckleheads continue their lame debate as they clean the kitchen."

Roman groans and stands collecting plates when I grab Dani's ass on the way to the living room. Dani starts some Christmas movie she's been dying to watch and we settle on the sofa together. I can hear the insults in the kitchen continue as plates clang. Then, Roman must say something really harsh because Andie shrieks.

"MY MOM IS DEAD YOU ASSHOLE!"

Dani and I both freeze.

"Oh shit," Dani says with a wince. "I worried this would happen when they started in on the mom jokes."

"HOW WAS I SUPPOSED TO KNOW?" Roman roars back. And then… "YOU BITCH!"

A series of grunts and splatters ensue before Dani and I can scramble off the sofa. We're just coming around the corner when a handful of spaghetti sauce splatters on Roman's no longer perfect white shirt. His face is red with fury and his chest heaves. He has another spot on his slacks. Meat and sauce decorate him and the floor. Andie has noodles hanging from her hair.

"You guys!" Dani chides in a shrill tone.

Andie glares at her over her shoulder. "He started it!" Then, she chucks another handful of sauce at him.

Roman lets out a growl and comes after her. He slips in the sauce, which causes him to tackle her to the floor. They both crash with a groan. And there is spaghetti shit everywhere.

"Oh. My. God," Dani murmurs.

We're both too stunned to move. Roman and Andie wrestle in the middle of the mess until he pins her wrists to the floor.

"I'm sorry, goddammit," he bites out.

Tears are quickly filling Andie's eyes. I start for the kitchen to get my brother off of her, but Dani grabs my arm and gives me a slight shake of her head.

"Well," Andie tearfully accuses. "You should be sorry. It's all your fault."

I give Dani a confused look and she simply shrugs.

"I didn't mean to hurt your feelings," Roman says lowly, his intense gaze on her.

"Then you should have called!"

Called? I'm totally missing something here.

Another growl from Roman. More confusion from me and Dani.

"You told me not to," he snarls, but then releases her wrist to gently pluck a noodle from her hair.

"Come on," I tell Dani. "I think they can sort this out on their own."

I grab her wrist and drag her down the hall to my bedroom. Once the door is closed, she sits on the bed, a frown on her face. I'm about to speak when I hear Andie shouting.

"PUT ME DOWN, YOU BIG OAF!"

"STOP SQUIRMING, GODDAMMIT. YOU'RE GOING TO GET SAUCE ALL OVER THE WALLS."

"I WANT TO GO HOME!"

"NOT UNTIL I CLEAN YOUR ASS!"

Dani's eyes widen when we hear the door to my brother's room slam shut. Then, I can hear the shower turn on. Andie screeches.

"IT'S FUCKING FREEZING, YOU DAMN

LUNATIC!"

My brother growls something too low for us to hear. Then, we hear banging around and something shatter. Dani rises to her feet and I quickly pull her in for a hug.

"He won't hurt her," I assure her. "I think they like to fight."

She relaxes in my arms. Andie continues to cuss him out. Then we hear…

"OH NO, BUDDY! PUT THAT THING AWAY! YOU ARE *NOT* GOING TO DISTRACT ME WITH THAT!"

Dani starts giggling and I shake my head. "Come on," I tell her. "Let's go clean the kitchen and then watch the movie. Maybe they'll have better attitudes once they've cleaned up."

Forty-five minutes later, Andie stomps into the living room wearing one of Roman's dark button-up shirts that hits her at the knees. Her hair is wet and messy, but she's clean. Either her cheeks are stained from the sauce or she's blushing. My smug brother comes sauntering in behind her, wearing jeans and a clean T-shirt and a shit-eating grin.

"Everything okay?" Dani questions from my lap. Her legs are draped over my thighs and she's curled up against my chest. I love having her in my arms.

"Fucking peachy," Andie tells her as she plunks down on the loveseat. Roman disappears into the kitchen.

Dani frowns at her friend. "Do you want me to take you home?"

Before she can answer, Roman reappears and hands

her a bottle of tequila. "I'm not done apologizing to her. She'll stay until she's happy again."

Andie glowers at him but accepts the bottle.

"You guys are good, though?" I ask my brother. "I don't need to send you to separate corners or anything?"

Roman chuckles. "I'm fine right here." He plops down onto the loveseat beside her. "So what's up? You guys down for a drinking game?"

I squeeze Dani's thigh. "Babe? You want to play a game?"

Dani shrugs. "As long as it doesn't end up with more crap we have to clean up, I'm good."

Andie bristles. "I'm not playing."

Roman pats her bare thigh. "You are." He turns to regard us. "It's called 'Most Likely.'"

Once he explains that everyone sits in a circle and one player asks a "most likely" question, like "Who would be most likely to stalk Ryan Gosling?" or "Who would be most likely to steal someone else's snack from the refrigerator at work?" on the count of three, everyone points to whoever they think would be most likely to do whatever act was mentioned. You have to take a drink for every person who's pointing at you. So if three people think you'd stalk Ryan Gosling, you have to take three drinks.

"We're going to need more alcohol," I tell them as I head for the kitchen and locate a few more bottles.

The game starts off with Andie still angry, but soon, everyone gets quickly drunk. Especially when Andie and Roman once again have a war, trying specifically to make the other drink.

"Who would be most likely to get drunk and fall

down a flight of stairs?" Andie slurs and then not so slyly points at Roman. Of course Dani and I encourage her by pointing to him too. He knocks back three shots of vodka and then flips us off.

Then Roman says, "Who would be most likely to win a wet T-shirt contest for the biggest tits in the room?"

Dani starts giggling so hard she falls off the sofa. We all know that even though her tits are sexy as hell, they're not as big as Andie's. Andie grumbles but takes her three shots of tequila.

This goes on and on until Andie gets mad at Roman again. She kicks him from her side of the loveseat. He growls and snags her ankle. Before I witness something that might scar me for life, I scoop up my clumsy girl, who's still on the floor, and make my way back to my room on wobbly legs. I manage to kick the door shut without falling with her in my arms. We tear at each other's clothes, which takes longer when inebriated, but eventually I have her naked and bent over the bed.

"God," I groan and rub my hard cock between her thighs. "I love looking at your ass."

She giggles against the covers and wiggles her butt at me. When I give her naughty ass a slap, she squeals.

"You like that, bad girl?" I demand, with a growl.

She fists the blankets and whines. "Mmmhhmmmm."

I grip my cock and slowly ease into her wet cunt. My girl is wet and ready for me. Always so fucking eager. I suck on my thumb and then tease her tight asshole. Normally, she's shy about when I try but tonight she's curious because she doesn't squirm away.

"You want me here tonight?" I question as I ease my

thumb into her tight hole.

"Oh God," she chokes out as her body quivers.

I work her into a frenzy with my thumb as I tease her pussy by sliding in and out of her ever so slowly. When she comes so hard I can feel her juices run down my balls, I slide out of her. My thumb pops out of her other hole and she makes a disappointed sound.

"Hold still, baby," I coo. My fist grips my still wet cock and I press against her puckered hole. Her body resists me with everything it has. "Relax," I order with a growl, pushing into her.

Her moan is one of pleasure, but also one of pain. I'm not sure if she's done this before, but by the way she's acting, I'd say not often. Despite my drunken haze, I still take care of her. Slowly but surely, I ease into her channel that grips my cock in a delicious way. Her pussy is heaven, but her ass is otherworldly. Once I'm all the way in, I settle one hand on her hip and slip the other one around her waist so I can touch her swollen clit. I don't move, despite my throbbing cock begging me to. Instead, I let her get acclimated to how it feels to have my massive dick filling her in such a delicate area. The more I massage her clit, the more she squirms. I don't move until she begs me to.

"Oh, God," she whines. "Ram, do it. Fuck me."

Jesus Christ, she is hot when she talks dirty.

"You sure, Buttercup?"

"So sure."

I thrust my hips and she screams. Over and over again, I pound into her until her entire body is shuddering as if she's been electrocuted. When her ass clenches tight around my cock, I come deep inside her.

"You…I…wow…" she trails off.

I chuckle and slip out of her gently. My cum runs out of her ass and down her inner thigh. "Come on. Let me clean you up in the shower, dirty girl."

She giggles when I scoop her up and make my way to the bathroom. Once I have her in the hot shower a few minutes later, I kiss her hard enough to make her knees buckle.

"Dani…"

Her hooded hazel eyes meet mine and she smiles. "Yeah?"

"I love you."

She hugs me and nods.

I guess she loves me too.

Chapter Thirteen

Dani

> ### It's Complicated

"SERIOUSLY, STOP LAUGHING!" THIS IS THE THIRD time I have had to tell Andie to control herself.

"I... I... I just can't." She barrels over laughing once again. This time I lose my patience with her, throwing down the sweater in my hands, and begin walking toward the exit of the department store.

"Okay! I'm sorry. I'll stop laughing. It's not funny. I swear." I whip around to see her fighting not to laugh again.

"I should've never told you. *Neither of those things,*" I stress, regretting trusting my best friend, who is trying not to laugh at my expense.

"Seriously. Yes. No. I mean *yes*! You should have. I'm your best friend and if you can't share your first anal experience with me then who *can* you share it with?" Her lips are twitching, fighting that damn smirk. I roll my eyes and turn back around leaving Miller's Department store. We came here to find ugly sweaters for our work party, and this has really been the first time since Friday that we had time to talk. Like, *really* talk. And stupid me told her about what Ram said to me. Then did to me.

"I'm sorry! Okay, listen. It's just that I've never had anyone explain anal like you did."

"Like how?" I ask incredulous.

"Dani, it took you three times to try and nonchalantly tell me what happened." She laughs. Again.

"I did not."

"You crossed the dark side?"

"Well, yeah." I shrug. I think it would be obvious.

"You then tried telling me Ram pinned the tail on the donkey." Her choked laughter works me back up.

"Well, I was trying to explain what happened. Kids are around! I didn't want to just blurt out I had sex in the butt!" A few on-goers stop and look our way. Andie busts out laughing back to her keeled over position while my cheeks burn with embarrassment. I turn and storm off.

"Oh Dani, come on! Don't be mad. This is exciting news! I'm not trying to discredit it. You took it in the back door. I'm so proud of you." I take a pair of slacks hanging on the nearest rack and throw them at her. She blocks it. "Honey, there's nothing to be embarrassed about. People stop, drop, and slip it in the wrong hole all the time." I halt and whip around.

"Would you stop it? I wish I never told you." I huff in frustration.

"Fine, you got to fifth base. Is that virginal enough talk

for you?" she questions, her blue eyes glittering wickedly. "But I mean technically anal is *far* from virg—"

Ughhh! I'm done. I turn and walk out of Millers into the busy evening traffic. I admit that that was the first time I'd ever done something so wild before. But it felt right. With Ram, everything does. Before Ram, I would have been disgusted if any other boyfriend would have tried that with me, but with him, it was exhilarating. Filled with passion and trust. I trusted him.

I knew it was going to hurt. I don't live under a rock. Well not *completely*. But I've heard Andie mention it enough times throughout the years to know it's an acquired taste. Once Ram got through my tightness, and my body adjusted, the erotic feeling of being filled in such a wicked way set my entire body in flames. The pain eased just as fast as the euphoric sensations kicked in. And when I came, it felt like I was flying. I've never orgasmed like I did with him inside me like that.

And the tenderness that followed was unspeakable. He washed me from head to toe, kissing every intimate place on my body. Once drying me, he laid me in his bed and just talked. He told me about his family. His dad, and how hard it was on him and both his brother and sister when he died. My heart hurt for him, his siblings, and his mother. From his stories, it sounded like his parents were madly in love. Rich in love, he called them. Ram's mother's side was very wealthy, her family coming from a huge inheritance. He explained that when his parents met, his mom's father did not approve of the coupling. Any parent, whose daughter was extremely wealthy already at such a young age, would guard their daughter against men who would only want her for her money. But Jacob, Ram's father, set to prove her father wrong. He told her father he didn't want any of her money. He wanted to provide for her himself. He loved her and that was his duty.

Almost thirty-five years of marriage and they never touched the money. Ram went into telling me that his dad had been high in the advertising world, and created an app that helped small businesses who couldn't afford their own marketing department. It took off instantly. He was able to market it to every small to medium-sized advertising agency in the northern region. Just as stage two of the app went live, his dad was diagnosed with cancer. He passed away not long after.

I held Ram through his sad words. He struggled with the loss of his dad the most, and shared with me that he still wasn't completely over it. I could tell he was hurting reliving the memories. I kissed his cheeks, his chin, his nose, showing him I was there for him. He flipped me and took my mouth in a forceful kiss telling me he was thankful. We made love, sweet and slowly. He was done sharing and I was okay with that.

We woke up to his phone ringing, his mother, who I could hear since she was yelling at him because she heard from Roman that he had a girlfriend. I giggled into Ram's chest while he tried to get a word in, but in the end, he just said, "Yes, Mom," agreeing to bring me over for dinner.

I didn't know why but I was all out of sorts knowing I had to meet his mom. What if she didn't like me? Doesn't approve of me dating her son? Andie always says that mothers are always crazy about their boys and to watch my back. She said once, she dated a guy whose mother would follow them to the restaurants spying on them to make sure she wasn't taking advantage of him.

What if his mom is a complete nutcase, I thought?

I left shortly after and called Andie. I needed advice. A lot had happened over the weekend and I needed to sort it all out. From the erotic sex, to him opening up to me, to his confession of love. Again.

God, I never said it back. I could tell he was hurt. But I was scared. I had these feelings raging inside me, and I knew they were too strong to hold in. I knew love was brewing long before he even confessed it.

Why I didn't say it back? I have no idea. I panicked. I would use the excuse that I wasn't sure, but I knew I was. I have never felt this way about someone before. Felt so grounded and full with love and trust. It hurt like hell that he lied to me, but I understood why. It made me feel guilty for making him think he had to. Because it wouldn't matter what he did. I would love him for him. And I did.

"Dani, wait!" Andie calls my name from behind, running to catch up to me. I didn't realize I had been power walking straight through town. "Stop! Seriously, I'm sorry. I'm an asshole. I know you're not me and take stuff like this more to heart. I love you. And I'm happy for you." I stop and turn to her. She looks out of breath. As much as I want to strangle her, she's my best friend and it's truly impossible to really be mad at her.

"Do people really refer to it as hide the pickle?" I ask, a small smile breaching my cheeks. She matches my humor, "You would be surprised at the list of nicknames."

And with that, it's water under the bridge. We walk to Eleanor's boutique to help me find something to wear for my dinner tonight with Ram's mom. I did get that much out before Andie went to town with her butt jokes. Since we had plans to go shopping for sweaters, she thought it would be fun to find me a new outfit, other than leggings and a bulky sweater.

"So wanna talk about the love comment?" she asks, handing me a black knee-length dress.

"I don't really know what to say. He said it. Then, I panicked and said thank you like an idiot. And it wasn't brought up again. He said it once more last night and I still didn't say it back." I take the dress and hang it back up on another rack since its way too short, and no way do I want his mom to think I'm a slut.

Handing me a red jumpsuit, she questions, "Did you *want* to say it back?" She grabs a necklace off a mannequin and holds it up to my neck. I push her away, afraid of what she might have me try on next.

"I think so."

"You think so? Dani, you do or you don't."

I take a deep breath, taking the purple tube top she just handed me and putting it back on the rack. "I wanted to say it back."

"Well, then why didn't you?"

"I have no idea! It's a big step."

"So is anal, but *holey moley* did that go just fine." I throw a scarf at her while she laughs and ducks.

"Sorry, but you set me up for that one," she says with a grin before becoming serious. "Honey, I've watched you the past few weeks and I have never seen you this way. If you needed any convincing, then I'm telling you. You're in love. And clearly, so is he. Love isn't always messy or

155

painful. Yeah, you've been hurt in the past, and yes, maybe you've said it in the moment to the wrong people, but this one? He's the one. I can tell. Put the poor guy out of his misery and admit what you already know." She hands me a pair of soft grey leggings, pairing it with an off-white fuzzy oversized sweater. "And let's stop wasting our time and put you in what we know you'll end up in." She winks. She knows me best.

We're pulling up a long driveway, a fancy, white two-story mansion coming into view, when I begin to feel even woozier than before.

"Babe, it's going to be fine. She's going to love you."

I attempt to adjust my hair for the millionth time. "Yeah and what if she doesn't. What if no one is good enough for her baby boy?" I turn to him, the fear in my eyes prominent. Ram just chuckles lifting our locked hands and placing a kiss to the top of my hand.

"She's going to love you. Trust me."

"And how do you know?"

"Well for starters, you're the first girlfriend I've ever brought home to meet her." Now *that* sends my anxiety through the roof.

"Oh God, Ram, pull over. I think I'm going to be sick."

He laughs again. "Too late. We've been sitting in the driveway for the past five minutes waiting for you to calm down. Can't turn back now. And look. She's already coming out to greet us." I lift my head to see a quaint little woman dressed in an adorable pair of black leggings and a grey oversized sweater with a sequined heart in the middle.

"She likes…" I trail off as I stare at her outfit.

"Like I said. She's going to love you." With one last smile, Ram hops out before walking over and opening my door. With no way to hide now, I reach for his offered hand and allow him to help me out of the Mustang.

"Oh heavens, you are just a sight," his mother says, moving past Ram, and wrapping me in a warm motherly hug. I lean in, shocked at her bold move. It's impossible to hide my stiffness, but once in her embrace, I smell her calming scent of vanilla. Her hands are warm, and before I know it, I'm wrapping my arms around her to return the hug. "There it is. Now, now." She releases me, turning to her son and swatting him in the chest. "And shame on you for hiding this precious little thing from me." Ram laughs, grabbing for his mother before she has a chance for further attack, bringing her in for one of his big bear hugs.

"Nice to see you too, Mom," he chuckles, placing a kiss into her hair. "Mom, I would like you to meet my girlfriend, Dani. Dani, this is my mom."

"Goodness, call me Virginia." I reach out and shake her hand, which now seems silly since we just got close and personal.

"Nice to meet you, Virginia," I reply nervously. "I love your outfit." *I love her outfit? Really Dani? Ugh.*

"And me, yours. It seems we have identical taste. You must tell me where you shop."

Ram shakes his head, pulling his mother and redirecting her toward the house. "Enough chatting out here. Dinner is probably ready and there's no sense standing out in the cold to get acquainted." Now it's my turn to smack Ram for being rude to his mom. He laughs, bringing me to his side, kissing the top of my head. We make our way inside Ram's beautiful childhood home. The entrance is as big as the house I grew up in. I expected, due to the size and beauty of the outside, for the inside to be just as pristine. The stereotypical mansion with tons of white marble and untouchable rooms. This was far from that. Family photos decorate every surface. It is warm and comfortable. A fireplace is lit in the family room and the television plays an old classic Christmas movie about Kris Kringle.

"Your home... It's so homey." I quickly cover my mouth, afraid I may have insulted her. "I mean, not that I would expect it not to be, it's just that, because, well..." *Shut up Dani.* Ram squeezes my hand while Virginia warmly smiles my way.

"I know what you mean. Jacob was all about family. He wanted his three children to grow up in a home filled with love and life." She leans in to me and whispers, "Unlike my parents' home. Very stuffy. All white. Couldn't touch a damn thing." My mouth drops as she repeats the exact thought I had just before. "Now come. Dinner is ready."

She pulls me out of Ram's grip and escorts me through the kitchen. The room is gigantic with what I can guess are all top-of-the-line appliances. Stainless steel with cabinetry from head to toe. The island is covered in dishes of all sorts, mashed potatoes, green beans, rolls, I feel like I could go on. She brings us through another entryway and into a cozy dining room, a large table filled to the brim with food.

"Wow. Who else is joining us?" I ask, wondering if she invited over half the town. Ram laughs, pulling out the chair for me.

"Nobody," he says with a chuckle. "My mother just loves to cook for an army."

Virginia smacks her son on the arm and takes her own seat. "That's true, but my boys also like to eat. I remember when they were younger, it was impossible to ever get them full. Poor Jacob and I thought we were raising wolves. Their metabolisms were off the charts." I look over at Ram, who's nodding, confirming what she said is true. "Reagan, despite being built like a pixie, can just about out eat those boys any day of the week. But Roman, he was my big eater. He played sports so you couldn't feed him fast enough before he burned it all off. And Ram…"

"I…well, I was just hungry." He smiles bright and wide. I take his hand under the table, and he threads his fingers between mine.

The rest of the dinner is wonderful. Virginia is kind and funny, and there is no doubt how proud she is of her boys and only daughter. When she speaks of her late husband the sadness is evident, but the love is so thick in her words, I catch myself wiping at my eyes. I can't remember the last time I ate such good food. And so much of it.

Virginia explained that after her husband died, she took up cooking as a hobby to keep busy. That, of course, was after she attempted knitting, piano, tennis, and scrapbooking. Cooking was a way to give her some happiness when she was missing her Jacob. That also found her cooking day and night. Since she was an empty nester nowadays and only got her kids over so often, she ended up packaging a lot of the food and bringing it to the local food pantries, helping on the weekends, or offering to families in need. On occasion, she flies out to see Reagan in California if their schedules allow.

I may have just admitted to myself that I am in love with Ram, but it took me less than an hour to admit I was also in love with his mother. She's sweet and funny. Kind in all aspects. We share the same taste in clothes and I find myself for the first time *ever* talking fashion with someone. The night is just amazing. Once dinner is over, Ram offers to clear the table, while Virginia grabs my hand and tells her son we will be in the study, getting an after-dinner drink. It confuses me since I thought that was a man's thing. Ram just gives me a kiss on the forehead and a wink before telling me to have fun.

"So, how is my baby boy really doing? He seems happy." She hands me a crystal flute filled with what looks like champagne. We both sit in two adjacent lounge chairs properly seated next to one another. Our view overlooks a large bay window. It's dark, so it's hard to tell what's out there, but I do notice it's begun to snow.

"I think he's happy too. Or at least I hope. He *seems* happy. I hope I'm making him happy." Let's see how many times I can use the word *happy* in a sentence. I turn to Virginia. "What I'm trying to say is…"

She waves me off. "I know what you mean. And he is happy. I haven't seen that side of Ram in ages. Years probably. Maybe even before his dad died." My heart hurts every time she mentions her husband.

"I'm sorry for your loss, really," I say, not because I feel I need to. Because I truly am.

"Oh, thank you, dear. Jacob was such a good man. Worked hard. Cared for his family. His company was his pride and joy, but his kids were his life. There was nothing he wasn't involved in. From sports, to school, to boyfriends and girlfriends. He made sure he knew exactly how his kids were being raised."

"He sounds wonderful."

"He was," she agrees, her eyes distant as she thinks about him.

Silence falls upon us. I think of my own parents who were just as loving in their own way. They were involved and caring, but as I grew up, I learned how sheltered they kept me. We didn't have much money so certain luxuries were never on our radar. My wardrobe was always basic, because that's what we could afford. I didn't get to go to any fancy colleges because it was too expensive. I didn't play sports because they were afraid I would get injured, but I'm sure cost was the main factor. They did make sure to teach me kindness and love. My daddy would always say that a giving person always receives the most in the end. I wasn't too sure what he meant, but ever since Ram came into my life, I feel like I get it now. He gives me so much more.

"How's the depression?"

Caught off guard, I turn and utter, "Huh?"

"Ram's depression."

Her question comes from left field. I didn't even know Ram *had* depression.

"I… I didn't know he suffered from it. I would have never… He's just always so… happy."

She smiles at me, lifting her hand and patting mine

that's resting on the armrest.

"Not too many people do. He's very private about it. He loved his dad. They spent a lot of time together. Wanted to follow him in his footsteps ever since he was little. So when he died, Ram took it the hardest. Started acting out. Stopped hanging out with friends. He stopped caring about college. He even dropped out for a while. We didn't hear from him for some time. He and his brother fought. Roman just wanted to help Ram. But to Ram, he was trying to take his father's place in his life. And Ram didn't want that. He wanted his dad. The only one who was able to really reach him was Reagan. She was about fourteen at the time and was the only person he'd talk to on the phone."

Being here has been an emotional roller coaster. From amazing stories to such sadness. Ram has depression. Why did he never tell me? I scrape my brain for anything that would have triggered it. Was he ever depressed with me? Did he ever show signs? Depression is not a small thing to keep to one's self. Being allergic to pets, maybe. But depression? Why would he keep this? Again, the fight we had about lying surfaces to the forefront of my mind.

"Either way. He looks healthy. And happy. How is my other baby? Still the mamma's boy he's always been?"

"Who?" I barely register her question, still lost in thought.

"Roman, my eldest but biggest baby."

"Oh, um, he's doing well, I guess. He's really busy, so I don't get to see him much." Or he's too busy battling Andie when we are all together.

"Now *that* boy. He may never find a girl. So needy.

162

Always wanting to find one just like his mamma."

At that I laugh, because Roman seems like a well put together businessman. Dominant, always in control. "I guess I never got that impression from him."

Virginia snickers, taking a hefty swig of her drink. "That boy would still have me do his laundry if I offered. He exudes this tough man persona, but he's a softy at heart. Still comes to his mamma for advice, and ohhhh-weee, when he gets sick. God help any woman he finally holds down. He will make you reconsider having children of your own. Huge baby." She winks at me, finishing off her drink. I do the same, and as I lay the empty glass on the coffee table, Ram enters.

"You two behaving? I hope my mother isn't telling you any embarrassing stories from high school." He leans over and presses a kiss to my lips. I can smell the mint gum and beer on his breath.

"Oh, you know, just telling Dani here how you sucked your thumb until you were twelve."

"I did not," Ram argues, but the gleam in his eye tells me otherwise.

"Either way, you—"

"MOM!" We all turn toward the opening of the study to hear Roman's voice booming through the halls. His large frame takes up the entire doorway, his stressed features prominent on his face.

"Oh, hello dear, I wasn't expecting you." Virginia smiles as she stands to hug her son.

"Sorry, I didn't mean to interrupt," he utters. "I just need to talk to you." Virginia smirks as if she knows that 'I need to talk' look.

"Sure thing, baby. Why don't we chat in the kitchen? I have a homemade pecan pie, your favorite. You can fill your sweet belly while we talk."

Ram and I both look at one another curiously, wondering what that is all about. Ram shrugs his shoulders, and after a few seconds, he grabs me, putting his finger over his mouth, telling me silently to be quiet. We tip toe to the kitchen and stand just outside the door as our ears perk to eavesdrop.

"But she is just out of control. How do I please someone who is so damn difficult?"

We both hear Virginia sigh, the sounds of the chair creaking as she sits. "Honey, women are delicate creatures. Sometimes you have to allow them to express who they are before trying to tell them what they should or should not want."

Roman scoffs. "Oh, this one knows exactly what she wants. She's like an untamed lion, with claws as sharp as knives, but then there is this soft side to her. Where she's just so… so… wonderful."

Ram throws his hand over my mouth when a small chuckle escapes my lips. "Shhh," he scolds me, that mischievous smile matching my own.

"I can't read her. It's like one minute I think we understand each other. And the next, she's trying to kill me. I don't know whether to kiss her or run for my life!"

At that, we both start laughing. Ram pulls us away from the doorway, dragging me back toward the study. "You busted us, you little minx you." He laughs, bending down and taking my lips in a playful kiss.

"Were you just eavesdropping?" We both turn to see

Roman, not looking as put together as normal. "What are you, five?"

Ram wraps his arm around my shoulder, bringing me close. "Sorry, we were just walking by and may have heard some things. I didn't know you were seeing someone."

"I'm not! I mean, I am. Sort of. Hell, it's just fucking complicated, okay?" He huffs, running his fingers through his thick hair. He grunts, then turns and storms out, griping over his shoulder, "Just mind your own business." We hear him say his goodbyes to Virginia and the slamming of the front door.

As Ram and I look at each other peculiarly, we both share the same conclusion that we might know exactly what or *who* his complication is.

Chapter Fourteen

Ram

> **Nice Try,
> Rameo**

"**Y**OU'RE GOING TO GIVE ME A DAUGHTER-IN-LAW." Mom's whispered giddy words keep replaying over and over in my head from the other night. Apparently Dani and I are solid stuff. *I* know it to be true but I'm glad others see it. Now, I just need to figure out a way to make Dani admit she loves me too.

"Where are we going?" Dani questions, giving my hand a squeeze.

I flash her a warm grin as we pull up to the outdoor mall. For her actual Christmas present, I'd already bought tickets to Silver Dollar City in Branson. I'm hoping she'll be excited to take a trip with me to Missouri. Tonight is more or less a date night. "We're going to spend the evening having some fun." We still have a week until Christmas, but I like dragging out her surprises so she gets presents every day.

Her pretty hazel eyes sparkle with wonder and I want to memorize her expression so that I can etch it permanently into my brain. Once we're out of the car, I smile as the brisk December air whips around us. I'm hoping, according to the forecast, that she'll get an extra surprise later. Dani clutches my hand, wearing a wide grin, as we make our way through the entrance that leads to all of the shops. She stops to gush over a window display with mannequins posed as if they are decorating a Christmas tree. Her smile is contagious and mine is never leaving as long as she's around.

"I love this place," she tells me with a giggle. "Andie hates coming here because you have to walk outside, but I love it."

She starts toward the first shop that carries hats, but I tug her away. A look of confusion crosses over her features when I guide her in the opposite direction. At first she seems disappointed, until we step into a pet shop.

"Oh my God!" she squeals and releases my hand to kneel in front of a gated area with kittens running wild. The worker laughs at her as Dani scoops up a black kitten into her arms. "He's so cute! Look how precious he is, Ram!"

I chuckle and kneel down beside her to pet the squirmy thing. Her smile is absolutely breathtaking as she nuzzles her cheek against him. We spend a good half-hour petting every single animal in the shop. Once I finally drag her out of there, she's on top of the world.

"I love them all!" she exclaims, clapping her hands together.

With a snort, I give her a teasing grin. "Well, cats are one of your *favorite* things."

Her eyes narrow at me, but this time she doesn't resist when I walk her toward a candy shop. In the front window, a worker stretches green taffy on one of their unique machines. Like a little kid, she stops and gazes in wonder. I swear we watch that machine go for a good twenty minutes before I'm able to get her to go inside. From there, she gets sucked in to sampling different flavors. Her thrill and excitement make me fall in love with her over and over again with each endearing smile. Once she's got a bag full of saltwater taffy and babbles on about how awesome it was, we leave the store.

"Saltwater taffy is one of my *favorite* things," she says, chomping on the candy.

I laugh and wink at her. "I know."

Her eyes do the narrowing thing again, but then we're off to our next destination. The ice rink is bustling with people but I'm only looking for one. When I hear a squeal, I know she's found us.

"Dani!" Andie screeches and nearly tackles my girl. "Tell me why I'm here to skate—which you know is my most *not* favorite thing in the world—and why I was told to dress like a ho!"

Dani bursts into laughter and doubles over, her dark hair falling in her face. Andie gives me a perturbed look, but I'm grateful she accepted the invitation. And as requested, she's dressed like she's ready to go clubbin' in a skintight dress. Luckily, she wore leggings underneath but her thigh high boots are totally hooker-ish and so is her furry white jacket. Her makeup is layered on thick and her blonde hair is a bouffant mess.

"Y-You're one of my *favorite* things," Dani giggles. "And so is skating!" She charges for me and throws her arms around my neck. "Ram, you're perfect."

I hug her tight and kiss the soft flesh of her neck. "So are you."

The girls skate a few laps while Andie bitches the whole time. I shoot my brother a quick text.

Me: <PHOTO ATTACHED> Girls' Night at the ice rink!

It takes Roman three seconds to reply.

Bro: What. The. Actual. Fuck. Is. She. Wearing?

Smirking, I ignore his text and continue to watch my girl and her best friend as they wobble over the ice. When Dani stops to come give me a kiss, I whisper in her ear. "You ready to ditch your friend and see the rest of your surprises?"

She laughs, but then frowns. "What about Andie?"

Smirking, I show her my text to Roman. "She'll have company soon."

My sweet girlfriend gives me a devilish look as she hurries to take her ice skates off. We abandon Andie and rush off to a stage that's off to the side of the rink. A bunch of children are on stage and are caroling. Dani's eyes shimmer with tears. I know I did well planning this all out for her. We make our way through the crowd of proud parents to the front. Song after song, Dani leans against me singing. My heart seems to expand larger than ever before. But when they start singing "White Christmas," my heart aches for my dad. Understanding washes over Dani because she gives me a peck on my cheek. "Christmas songs are my *favorite*. I'm ready for my next surprise, though."

With a sad smile, I leave the area so I can put that memory behind me. I've been watching the time but my next surprise hasn't happened yet. I frown in disappointment until I feel something cold hit my cheek.

I stop dead in my tracks and pull her into my arms. "Look up."

She looks up in wonder as if I had the magical ability to make it snow just for her. Snowflakes dot her pretty face, and again, I wish for the ability to burn this moment into my mind forever. When her shimmering eyes meet mine again, she mouths the words *thank you*. I give her a nod as if it's no big deal before sliding my palms to her cold cheeks. Our lips meet softly at first, and then I kiss her deeply in front of the crowded shoppers. Her tongue is sweet like the taffy, and I crave to taste her all night long. Someone, who sounds an awful lot like Roman, yells, "GET A ROOM!" and we break away.

"Come on," I tell her, "I have another surprise for you."

She beams at me as I drag her to the vintage comic shop. I'd called ahead to make sure they had what I needed. As soon as we make it inside, we cough a little on the haze of incense before Dani gets lost thumbing through used DVDs. I leave her to get my hold from behind the counter that I paid for over the phone. When I make it back over to her, I hold out my present.

"Oh, Ram," she says softly and takes the box set from me.

"It's only the first season of *ER* but I thought we could

keep it over at my place since you've been spending time over there a lot. I know it's your—"

"*Favorite*," she interrupts, her gaze fiery. I could almost bet if people weren't here, she'd jump me right here in the aisle.

"You ready for more?" I question, wagging my eyebrows at her.

She stands on her toes. "I don't deserve more."

This time, it's me giving her the fierce gaze. "You deserve everything."

I press a soft kiss to her lips and grab her hand. She's quiet as we make our way to JC Penney's. As soon as we walk inside, she starts bouncing.

"You didn't," she says in a giddy tone.

"It's your *favorite*," I tease as I guide her over to the home section. The towels are an absolute nightmare as shoppers have made a mess shopping for last-minute gifts. Dani shoves all of her bags into my hands and runs over to the first pile she sees. I lean against a shelf with my hip and watch her as she starts folding towels as if it's her job. For a half-hour she does this. She makes the whole section neat and color-coded. She answers shoppers' questions with glee. In this moment, she's so fucking cute I can't even stand it.

"Oh my God," she whines, forcing herself to step away from another display. "Folding towels is my *favorite*."

I laugh and slap her sexy little ass. "Yeah, yeah. Let's keep going. I have more."

She squeezes my hand as I guide her out of the store and back outside. I lead her over to a kiosk in the middle of the breezeway that sells smoked sausage and—

171

"CHEESE!"

Chuckling, I peer with her at the impressive selection. The worker offers her some samples, and she scrunches her nose as she attempts to decide which tastes best. Eventually, she decides the pepper jack cheese is the winner, and I buy her a block of it.

"I can't believe you've done all of this," she says, shaking her head in disbelief. "Who knew a wrong number could go oh-so-right?"

I wink at her. "You hungry?"

She nods. "Famished. But I still don't understand how you'll find me my last favorite thing."

Shrugging, I guide her through the throng of people toward the restaurants at the end. There are some higher end places like PF Chang's and Olive Garden. There's even a steakhouse that certainly isn't in the budget. But none of those are what I want. Before we get there, she stops at an ornament shop. Her cheeks turn bright pink as she regards me with hooded eyes.

"Can you wait here for a minute?"

Flashing her a crooked smile, I nod. "For you, I'd wait forever."

She lets out a sweet sigh before disappearing into the store. It takes more like twenty minutes, but I promised her many more than that. Eventually, she comes out with a triumphant grin and a bag in her hand. I don't ask what's inside because it's clearly for me.

"Ready?" she questions.

I offer my elbow, to which she takes. We stroll past some restaurants that smell like heaven until we get to Cracker Barrel.

"Cracker Barrel?" she asks, her nose doing that cute scrunching thing again.

I point at several white-headed people rocking in the chairs out front. "Old people."

She snorts with laughter and punches me in the arm. "Oh my God, Ram!"

"It's one of your *favorite* things," I say in defense. "And you know I can't deny you a thing, baby. Especially not your favorite things."

Dani then kisses me hard enough to make every single one of those old people blush.

"Here, okay?" Dani questions as she holds a glittery faux icicle.

"Does it really matter?"

She rolls her eyes. "Duh! Your tree needs to be perfect."

I chuckle and admire my woman who looks sexy as hell with her hip cocked to one side. Her dainty hand is firmly placed on one hip, red and white striped polish on her nails.

"Babe, it's the first time Roman and I have ever put up a tree. It could be missing all the ornaments and still be better than we could have ever done on our own."

She huffs and hangs the icicle. "I want you to smile every time you see it."

"I smile every time I see you," I retort.

Her eyes cut over to mine and she chews on her plump bottom lip. My cock lurches in my pants, fully knowing what she can do with those lips.

"Come here," I tell her, my voice husky.

She abandons her decorating for a moment. "Why?"

"I want to hold you."

"Does this holding end with me naked?" Her dark eyebrow is arched in question, but she keeps walking toward me.

I lift an eyebrow back at her. "Do you want it to?"

The pink on her cheeks is a dead giveaway. "No." Lies.

"Mmmhhhmm," I placate, but offer my hand.

She clutches it and climbs onto my lap, straddling me. I love that she wears these thin leggings all the time because it allows me to feel all of her sweet, soft spots unlike jeans. My palms caress her round ass as her fingers thread into my hair.

"Your bags are gone." Her eyes are narrowed as she inspects me.

I drag my gaze over to the shopping bags from earlier that are discarded on the coffee table. "Did you lose one?"

Her thumbs slide under my eyes. "These bags. You're sleeping more, huh?"

My lips lift on one side. "I sleep when I'm happy. *You* make me happy."

The sadness that seemed to flash in her eyes melts away as relief takes over. "You make me happy, too," she assures me. "In fact…I…well, you see…I lo—"

A buzzer goes off in the kitchen and she scrambles off my lap. I watch her ass jiggle as she runs into the kitchen to pull out the cookies she was making. Eventually, she returns with a plateful of chocolate chip cookies warm from the oven. She fusses over me and won't let me feed myself. I watch her with heated eyes as she delicately breaks off soft pieces and puts them in my mouth. Her serious expression fades to amusement when I bite her finger.

"I'm hungry for something sweeter," I tell her with a growl. "You should take off your pants and let me suck on your clit for a while."

"RAMSEY!" she shrieks and slaps at me. But my girl, ever the horny one, climbs off my lap and starts giving me a striptease to "Santa Baby" which happens to be playing in the background. When she's good and naked, she continues to dance, a wicked grin on her face. Eventually, she sits beside me on the sofa and teases my mouth with her toe. Dani is so unguarded in this moment. So brave and curious. So fucking trusting. I grip her ankle and suck on her toe until she squeals. Then, I push her leg until her knee is against her chest. Her silky pink pussy glistens with her arousal. I wasn't lying when I said I was hungry for her.

I'm fucking ravenous.

I let out a growl of eagerness as I dive into my delightful treat. Her fingers grip at my hair and a low moan escapes her the moment my hot breath tickles her cunt. Using my thumbs, I rub at the outer lips of her pussy before pulling them aside so I can see her clit. It looks swollen and needy for attention so I give it a little nibble before I suck on it as promised. Her moans are no longer quiet but more like lioness growls. She squirms and groans with every swirl of my tongue.

"So fucking sweet," I praise as I sink my tongue into her hot center. She's tight as hell, even on my tongue. My cock aches to take its place.

"Rammmmmmm....."

I continue to suck and nibble on every part of her perfect pussy until she's saying my name like a chant. Her body shudders with her orgasm. I make sure to suck on her clit extra hard to make it last a little longer. When she's over sensitized, she pushes me away.

"Inside," she murmurs. "Now."

I smirk at her and lick my lips, enjoying the scorching way she stares at me. Her eyes follow my hands to the bottom of my black fitted Henley and then settle on my chest the moment I peel it away. "Like what you see?" I tease.

She nods. "I think so, but I'm afraid I'll need to see more to have a more definitive answer."

I give her a smug look as I unbuckle my jeans. When I go too slowly, she sits up and takes over. The woman practically undresses me like I'm a child. I laugh until she pulls me on top of her.

"I should get a condom," I tell her, my hard dick sliding against the wet lips of her pussy but not entering her.

She whines and clutches my cock. "Just come on my belly."

Our eyes meet for a heated moment before I slowly inch into her tight heat. We haven't been exactly responsible sexually, but with Dani, it doesn't really matter to me. I love her. I see myself with her in ten, twenty, fifty years. I'm going to marry this girl one day. And I'll put fifteen damn babies inside of her, if that's what she wants.

"Ram," she hisses, when I sink fully into her. She's a small woman, so it always takes her a minute to adjust to the size of my cock. Once her arousal has coated my dick, I'm able to slide in and out of her more easily. "Faster," she urges. Her fingernails dig into my shoulders.

I piston my hips into her powerfully, enjoying the way she moans loud enough to irritate the neighbors. Grabbing a handful of her hair, I thrust into her hard and fast like she keeps begging for. Our lips meet, no longer sweet, and we kiss furiously. I can't seem to get enough of her. I want all of her…and then some more.

Her body, still worked up from her last orgasm, begins to tighten around me. Short breaths escape her between kisses as she begins to unravel. I groan when her cunt hugs my cock.

"I'm going to come," I growl and start to pull out.

She digs her heels into me to hold me still. My eyes close as pure bliss ripples through me. I let out a hiss the moment my cock starts throbbing out its release. Sure, we're being irresponsible, but apparently she doesn't care either.

You don't sleep with someone without birth control unless you love them. She loves me. I know this. No matter how much I want them, I don't need the words. I can feel them even when she doesn't say them.

My heat spills completely into her and I collapse on her tiny frame. She plants gentle kisses along my jaw. "Ram…I…"

I hold my breath, waiting for the words.

"I…I need more eggs. For the cookies." Her words are shaky, as if she's disappointed in herself.

I lift up and give her a warm grin that doesn't quite reach my eyes. "You get cleaned up and finish decorating. I'll run out and grab us some, Buttercup."

Her frown lifts into a smile. "You're my new *favorite* thing. We can take Andie off the list," she teases.

I give her a chaste kiss before sliding out of her hot body. The evidence of our lovemaking trickles out the moment I pull out. "I'll be right back and we can pick up where we left off."

She steels her features and glances over at her bag on the table. Determination flashes in her eyes. "Yes. Perfect. Get the eggs and then I have a surprise for you."

An evil grin quirks up my lips. "Should I get canned whipped cream and cherries too? Is this an edible surprise?"

Her laugh fills the room as she chucks my shirt at me. "Nice try, Rameo. Your surprise is much sweeter."

I lift my eyebrows in surprise. "Cunt for second dessert? And here I thought I was only going to get to taste that pretty pussy once tonight."

"RAM!" she shrieks, heat turning her cheeks a dark shade of red.

Smirking, I gather my clothes up and head toward the bathroom to clean up. "We're going to continue this cuntversation later. I'll get you to say that word yet. Mark my words."

She runs after me and bounds into the bathroom on my heels. "No siree, Bob! Not ever. That horrible word is *not* in my vocab!"

I pull her naked body against me and give her a wolfish grin. "Want to make a bet?"

"Hmm. A bet against the tricky Ramsey. I don't know," she teases.

"We have a cuntversation where you use the *horrible* word," I tell her, and then tug at her lip with my teeth. "And then I'll eat that pretty cunt every night for dinner for a week."

"Seems like a winning bet. And if I don't say the *horrible* word?" she taunts.

I grab her bare ass and lift her up before setting her on the edge of the counter. My dick is hard again, rubbing against her still dripping sex. "If you don't, then you won't get my naughty little tongue ever again."

She huffs. "Hardly seems fair."

With a smirk, I push inside of her, enjoying the way her fingernails claw at my shoulder. "Whoever said I play fair?"

Chapter Fifteen

Dani

> ## Stop Being
> ## so Naïve

WATCH THE DOOR SHUT BEHIND HIM AND I WANT TO run after him. *I need more eggs? Really, Dani?* I cover my face with my hands, shaking my head. I should run out and stop him. Save him from the trek to the convenience store in the snow. It's started to come down pretty heavily now and we are forecasted to get almost a foot of snow by midnight.

I walk over to the coffee table, where I dropped my bags, and shuffle through them until I find the one I'm looking for. I gently pull out the ornament I had made for Ram and I stare at the personalization.

I love you.

-Dani

The simple, round ornament, shiny red in color and filled with glitter and happiness, stares back at me. I guess *myself* knew I would be too chicken to say it out loud, so thankfully I thought quickly. The second I saw the shop I knew what I wanted to do. I roll the ornament in my hand, the excitement building inside me. I'm going to tell him I love him.

"*Hi Ram, I love you… Ram, guess what? I love you too… I love you, where should we put the star*?" I giggle to myself, twirling around his living room. The reflection of the ornament catching on the light. I smile big, the fullness in my chest for how much in love I am. Ram makes me feel so many things, love is just the start. I dance around the tree repeating the words, *I love you, Ram*, laughing and smiling like an idiot. The jingling of the door handle perks my ears and I panic, putting the ornament on the tree. I turn just as the door opens, but it's neither Ram, nor Roman.

"Oh… hello?" I stare at a stranger. A woman. Not just any woman, but a drop-dead-gorgeous runway model type of woman. She's as tall as Ram but very delicate and refined. Her smooth chocolate-colored skin is pretty against her white suede coat. Dark brown eyes encased in long black eyelashes blink at me in confusion. Her full lips part as if she wants to say something, but then she presses them closed and frowns at me.

I stare at her stupidly.

Once she seems to pull herself together from the shock of seeing me, her features harden and she lifts her chin in the air slightly. With narrowed eyes, she takes my appearance in with one quick dismissive glance.

"Yeah, uh, I was looking for Roman. And *who* are you exactly?" Her cruel attitude does not go unnoticed.

I bristle at her words. "I'm Ram's girlfriend. And you?" I reply, sounding unsure for some strange reason.

Her brows raise and her eyes widen at my statement. "Pardon me but did you say girlfriend?" She steps closer into the apartment, causing me to step back. Who is this girl and why does she have a key to Ram's place?

"You're telling me *you're* Ram's girlfriend?" she asks again, as if not believing me the first time.

"I am, and you still haven't said who you are," I bite back with a little more backbone this time.

She snickers at me, but not in a polite way. "I, honey, am the one before you. Used to date Ram, well until his secret got exposed. Must have a strong stomach to want him after his disgusting addiction." She pauses, her eyes taking me in. "Must be why he chose someone so... mousy. Boring on the eyes." She practically *tsks* at me. Her insult hits me right where she plans, causing my hands to go up, adjusting my sweater. What secret? And he never mentioned dating someone before me.

"I'm not sure what you're talking about exactly. Why are you here?" I ask again.

Her eyes gleam with distaste and her smile is anything but friendly. "You don't know, do you? Tsk tsk, Ramsey. Always keeping secrets. Well, I guess I would too if I got outed for my kiddie porn obsession and fired from work."

I can't even fight back the horrible gasp that leaves my throat. "Excuse me?" I ask, my voice immediately shaking.

Her laughter is like acid washing over me. "That's right, little girl, *porn*. Got caught with it all over his work computer. I mean, at work? Couldn't even wait to get home? Shame. He had an amazing cock. But no dick is worth that sick shit. Well, maybe if you were desperate for a man." Her eyes skitter over my body, throwing the insinuation at me.

My stomach turns like a tidal wave, the cookies threatening to expel. My face has surely lost all color. Child pornography? It can't be true. "I don't believe you," I say weakly.

"Don't really care if you do. But it's true. Ask Roman. Fired his own brother himself. Had to have been hard for him. And the embarrassment he held? Good thing I was there to console him. Been there for him ever since." She pulls her eyes away from me to look around the apartment. "He sadly stormed out of work on Friday so I wanted to make sure he was okay. You know. Cheer him up if he needed it." Bringing her eyes back on me, she winks before licking her collagen-filled lips. "Well, tell Roman I came by." She smacks her lips once more, before swaying her hips and exiting where she came from.

I'm disgusted and hurt and sick. My chest is heaving, my head spinning with words I can barely process. Child pornography, fired…

My shaky hands grab for my stomach, the sharp pains causing me to buckle over.

Child pornography.

The world around me begins to spin. He couldn't. Ram isn't like that. He wouldn't. *He never told you why he was fired.* No, no no. "Oh God." I need to leave. I cannot be here when he returns. I pull myself together as I frantically search for my things. I grab my jacket, knocking over the chair it was hanging over, and shove my feet into my boots. I trip over the pile of bags all over the living room that I'd strewn while looking for the ornament and fall into the wall. I'm starting to struggle to breathe, the panic attack brewing heavily inside me.

How could he do this? His lies. He promised never to lie to me. But this is bigger than lies, it's a secret that affects us both. He made me fall so madly in love with him and he kept such a huge secret from me. I shake my head furiously. *You don't know if this is true.* That hateful woman had jealousy seeping from her evil eyes. Anyone could see that. She could be lying to me. No way could Ram be into something so horrendous. *Stop being so naïve.* Oh God, could he, though? My stomach contracts again at the thought. I make it out and into the heavy snow before I turn, bending over and emptying my stomach.

Taking three big gulps of the frigid air, I allow myself just enough time for the dizziness to pass and then I am running. I slip twice before I make it to my car. It takes me three attempts before my shaking hands get the key into the ignition. I don't even wait for the windshield to defrost before I take off.

Child pornography.

No.

I don't believe it. That's not Ram.

Then why did you just run?

"No, no, no, no!" I slam my fists on the steering wheel. Why did he lie to me? After our fight, I told him no lies. He could have come out then. Told me it was all lies. But he didn't. Because maybe he couldn't.

I shake my head furiously. No. This can't be happening. This is *not* happening. I'm repeating myself frantically, the snow coming down thick and fast. I know I'm driving way too fast for the slick roads, but I need Andie. I need her to tell me this is all a bad dream. Trying to watch the road, I fire off a quick text letting her know I'm coming over.

Child pornography.

Lies.

"Damn you, Ram!" I close my eyes tight as I scream. My car hits a patch of ice, but when I pop my eyes open, it's too late. The car spins out of control. I attempt pressing on my brakes, but it only accelerates the tailspin. I see the snow bank ahead and with no way to avoid it, I close my eyes and brace for impact. The car slams into the snow bank, jolting my body forward. My head slams into my steering wheel, causing a wave of dizziness to rush through me. I take a few minutes to catch my breath as I look around. There's a sharp pain coming from where my forehead hit the steering wheel and I raise my hand. Wincing as I pull back, my white glove is now red. Oh great. I pull my visor down to see a small gash in my forehead and I break down.

I cry.

My sobs are so powerful. I begin to choke on each attempt to suck in air. A knock on my window startles me, and I look to see an old man standing outside my car. I take in a deep breath and roll down my window.

"Excuse me, miss, are you okay?"

"Yes, I'm fine. Thanks."

"Are you sure? You're bleeding."

"Yes. Have a good night." I roll up my window and find a tissue in my center console, dabbing at my forehead. It takes me a few attempts to pull my car away from the

185

snow bank, and then I numbly drive with more care to Andie's. I barely remember the short drive. I jump out, almost forgetting to put the car in park, and race into her building. I dig into my purse for my keychain and locate the key I have for her place. It causes a realization to practically smack me in the face. That woman had a key.

She had to be someone special to Ram to have a key to their place. Something he's never offered me. My lower lip is quivering uncontrollably. The tears flowing down my cheeks are clouding my vision, making it hard to get the key into the lock. "Come on, come on…" I don't want to break down in the hallway or be caught by any of her tenants. Finally, the key slips in and I push her door open. "Andie?" I cry out. I'm met with a deep groan, causing my vision to veer toward the couch and—

"Oh my God!"

"Oh, fuck."

Before I have a chance to cover my eyes, I take in a completely naked Roman rising from the couch. "Oh my God! I'm so sorry," I shriek. Andie's head pops up, her eyes wide with shock.

"Oh fuck. Shit! This isn't what it looks like!" Andie spits out.

"What do you mean, this isn't what—"

Roman doesn't get to finish. Andie pushes him off her, causing him to lose his balance. I yelp as he tries to stand, his gigantic manly parts in full view as he trips and falls backward over the side of the couch. Mortified, I turn preparing to leave.

"Dani, no wait," Andie calls after me. "Seriously, get dressed and get the fuck out of here," she scolds Roman.

When I turn back around, it's just in time for him to offer Andie a scathing glare before then turning around so I don't have to see his impressive junk anymore. His tight bare butt cheeks clench as he walks toward the bathroom.

"Oh God." I cover my eyes, forgetting the wound on my forehead, and wince. Pulling my hands away, I see Andie throwing on an oversized T-shirt and coming at me.

"Holy shit, Dani. What the fuck happened?" She goes to reach for my cut, but I swat her hand away. "Who did this to you? Did Ram do this?!"

"My brother would never lay a hand on a girl," Roman argues, walking back, now wearing a pair of jeans, but missing his shirt.

"Dude, no one asked you," Andie snaps. "And why don't you have a fucking shirt on?!"

"Because you're wearing it!" he yells back at her.

She huffs, turning her attention back on me. "Honey, what happened?" Her tone is gentler, her eyes shining with concern. I try to speak, but I just start to cry.

"I… I… w-was at Ram's…"

"I KNEW IT! That bastard."

"He wouldn't do that." Roman steps forward.

They start going at it, and I step in. "Some w-w-woman… c-came over…"

Roman stops staring down Andie, and turns to me. "Wait, what woman?" he asks. "When?"

"S-s-she didn't tell me her name. She was tall, mocha skin, and beautiful and…"

"Chelsea," Roman states. So they do know her. My heart constricts, my lungs struggling to get in air at each attempted breath.

"She s-said some horrible t-t-things…" I can't continue. The sobs are restricting my words.

"What did she—"

"Jesus, why are you still here? Get out!" Andie cuts him off.

"You have my shirt," he growls at her. Andie looks around until she spots his jacket. Picking it up, she tosses it at him and says, "You're a big boy, I'm sure you won't freeze… Sadly." They go into an uncomfortable stare down until Andie has enough and kicks him hard in the shin.

"JESUS, WOMAN!" Roman yells, but Andie opens the front door and pushes him out. "Take a hint, dude." And once he's fully outside, she slams the door in his face.

"Seriously, I have no idea why he was here." She shakes her head.

"Andie, really, you don't have to—"

"For real, I can't stand that guy. Fuckin' stalker."

I open my mouth to argue, but I just shut it.

"Honey, talk to me. You look horrible and that cut looks bad. What happened?"

I don't automatically tell her what's happened. I fall into her arms and cry until we find ourselves both on the floor while she holds me. "Dani, you're starting to scare me. I know you're upset, but you need to tell me something." I proceed to, as best I can, tell her about my night. How perfect Ram was, the tree, how in love I felt. I told her about the ornament and my plans, and then how Ram left to get eggs when the woman, Chelsea, showed up.

"Does Ram know why you left?"

"No, I couldn't face him. I just left."

"That's some crazy shit, girl. I would never pin Ram as a kiddie porn lover." I start to cry again at her statement. Because neither would I. Even after, I'm still unsure. But even if I asked, how would I know he was telling the truth?

"Oh, Dani, I'm so sorry. This is so messed up. I really don't know what to say. It's disgusting, but I don't know. This bitch kinda seems, from how you described her, jealous. Do you think she was just saying it to get you to break up with Ram?"

I lift my head off her shoulder, feeling disgusted with what I have to tell her. "Andie, she told me that she is with Roman now. That's why she was there." I hate myself for having to hurt my best friend, but she needs to know. A look of hurt, then betrayal shines bright in her eyes.

"That fucking asshole," she says calmly.

"I'm sorry. But I thought, if you two were—"

"We weren't. Like I said…" she trails off, doing a horrible job of hiding her disappointment. I hug her again, needing the comfort of my best friend. I start to cry again because I can't stop replaying what happened. Andie convinces me that it's best we go to the ER and get my head checked out, and possibly stitches. I refuse at first, but the pain throbbing in my forehead tells me it is wise to do so.

"I'll drive this time," she says, trying to make light of my horrible, under duress, driving skills.

Chapter Sixteen

Ram

> **It's Beginning To Feel A Lot Like Fuck You**

WITH THE CARTON OF EGGS TUCKED UNDER MY arm, I whistle as the elevator ascends to my floor. Dani was so cute earlier. Her pasty white cheeks were ruddy with color when the words dangled at the tip of her tongue. Words I knew she wanted to say. Words I craved to hear. And true to Dani, she bailed because she couldn't quite find the words. I'm not bothered, though, because she didn't have to say them. They were glittering in her hazel eyes. I felt them down to my toes.

I push my key into the door and push through. Christmas music is playing a lively song and the loft smells of chocolate chip cookies. I'm dying to pull Dani into my arms and hold her while we watch a movie. Seems like whenever she's not around, my world is empty. Her smile, her heart, her laughter—they all fill me up with a happiness I've never known before.

"Honey," I sing as I put the eggs into the fridge. "I'm home."

I hear a soft feminine voice from my bedroom. A chair has fallen over and I pick it up, frowning in confusion. Shopping bags are strewn all over the floor. My heart aches as a sense of foreboding settles over me.

"Babe?" I call out. "Everything okay?"

Again, the voice from my room.

Stalking through the living room, I make my way toward my bedroom. The door is cracked and the room is dark inside. I feel as though my heart is going to beat out of my chest. This heavy, unsettled feeling threatens to make me sick. As soon as I push into my dark bedroom, it closes shut behind me. Then, Dani's soft hands slide up under my leather jacket, her fingernails digging into my flesh. I let out a sigh of relief as I turn in her arms. When I bend to meet Dani's lips, I'm met with a bare collarbone that smells hauntingly familiar. This person is taller. Bonier. Not my girlfriend.

No.

"What the fu—"

"Shhh…."

Bile rises in my throat as pieces begin to snap together. This is not Dani. This is fucking Chelsea. With a hiss of fury, I jerk from her grip and fumble for the light switch. When the light shines upon the bare brown flesh of my ex-girlfriend, I freeze.

"Why the hell are you in my loft, Chelsea? And furthermore, where is my girlfriend?" I seethe, bending to snatch up her clothes that she discarded on the floor. I sling them at her, and then run my fingers through my hair in frustration. "What did you say to her, goddammit?"

Chelsea sneers and begins hastily dressing. At one time, this would have been all I wanted. Maybe three or four months ago when I was at an all-time low with my depression. Had Chelsea showed up and apologized back then, I'd have taken her back in a heartbeat. I thought I loved her. Now that I have Dani, I understand that what I had with Chelsea was severe infatuation. She was beautiful and fearless and successful. Chelsea knew what she wanted out of life—me and her father's company. But then I was no longer on that list of wants for her. I was discarded the moment she got bored.

"Chelsea," I growl in warning. She stuffs her feet into her heeled boots after getting dressed and points a manicured nail at me.

"I told her about your little addiction." Triumph gleams in her eyes.

I'm going to be sick. "I don't have an addiction," I snarl, my hands fisting with the need to pummel the walls. "You set me up!"

She shrugs her shoulders as if sending that shit to me and it getting me fired wasn't a big deal. Any other company would have investigated further. But when your daddy is the owner, things go differently. She let them believe I was a monster...and I didn't argue otherwise.

"Ramsey," she tells me, waltzing over to me as if it's no big deal she's potentially ruined my life again. "I simply told her what you failed to. Secrets really are a problem for you, aren't they? You just try and hold on to them until you die. Some people hate secrets. I, for one, like them. Like our little secret…the one you hold on to still. It's sweet. Romantic even. Shows how much you still love me."

"I DON'T LOVE YOU!" I roar back in frustration. "Give me my damn key and get the fuck out of my house."

She huffs and locates the key before slamming it down on my desk with a clang. "I didn't come to see you. I came for your brother."

Sickness bubbles up inside me and rage overwhelms me. "Leave. Stay the fuck away from my girlfriend. Stay the fuck away from my brother. And for the love of God, stay the fuck away from me."

She glares as she storms off. Before she exits my room, she laughs. "Well, technically she's not your girlfriend anymore. Bye, Ramsey."

As soon as the apartment door slams shut, I bolt from my room, digging my phone out of my pocket along the way. I knew something was off when I came back. The tipped over chair. Dani's missing purse. Bags all over the floor. Everything seemed to be abandoned in haste. I should have listened to my gut. I'm dialing Dani as I scoop up my keys and rush out the door. It rings and rings and rings. Voicemail after voicemail, I beg for her to call me back—that it isn't what she's thinking.

But I lied.

And if I know my girl, which I do, she's less concerned about the accusations and more concerned with the fact that I kept the entire situation from her.

Why the fuck didn't I just tell her why I was fired? She all but asked and I toed very delicately around the issue. Sure, I didn't blatantly lie to her but I lied by omission. She flat out told me lying was a deal breaker for her.

Fuck!

I beat my fist against my steering wheel as I attempt to drive carefully through the snow while also trying to hurry. It takes twenty minutes longer than usual to get to her apartment. When I finally make it up to her unit, she's not there. I beat on the door for a good few minutes and can even hear her cat, Marilyn Manson, meowing on the other side but nothing else.

Fuck! Fuck! Fuck!

I've missed a couple of calls from Roman but I can't deal with him right now. I need to find Dani and explain this whole mess. I need her to forgive me. Once I'm back in the car, I head over to Andie's. Dani and I went there once to pick her up for dinner, and I still remember the way. With each passing moment, I grow more and more frantic. I can't lose her. Not now. Not after everything. We're in love and I can't let that get thrown away over such a stupid thing I did.

Once I get to Andie's building, I nearly fist pump the air when I see Dani's car. I slip and slide into the building before bounding up the stairs, unable to wait for the elevator. By the time I reach her door, I'm doubled over and out of breath.

"Andie! Is Dani here? I need to see her!" I shout as I pound the door.

Nothing.

Crickets.

I beat and beat until I realize they're not here. She had to have gone off with Andie somewhere. *Jesus fuck!*

Dialing Dani's number, I bite my fist while I wait for

her to answer. So many emotions filter through me. Anger at myself. Hate toward Chelsea. Bitterness over the unfairness of it all. Loss and heartbreak over Dani.

I'm just dialing her for the umpteenth time again when Andie calls me. I quickly answer it.

"Let me talk to her—"

"You listen here, asshole," Andie cuts me off, her voice cold and harsh. "You lied about some pretty epic shit. Kiddie porn, Ram? Fucking really?"

"Listen. You don't underst—"

"No! My friend can't deal with you right now. If she ever wants to hear your sorry excuses, she'll contact you. Stop bothering her. It's over, Ram. Over."

"Andie, please."

"Just hang up." Dani's hiccuped sob in the background slices through me like a hot knife.

"Andie—"

"Goodbye, Ram."

Minutes. Hours maybe. Days. I'm not sure how much time has passed since I heard her voice through Andie's phone. She was broken. I broke her. And now I don't know how to fix us.

My bedroom is dark and I stare up at my ceiling, still fully clothed. I can't stop imagining scenarios of how Chelsea and Dani's conversation went down. Each one, though, I see her crushed expression and it whittles away at my heart. If I keep obsessing over this, pretty soon, my heart will be nothing but a pile of shavings just waiting for the next breeze to blow away and scatter them.

The front door swings open and I hear Roman stomp into the house. His tells are always the same. Heavy footsteps. Doors slamming. Keys and briefcase and whatever other shit he carries around with him getting dropped and discarded along the way. Normally, he bypasses my room to go to his. Tonight, though, he knocks on my door.

"Ram?"

I don't respond.

He pushes through the door and switches on the light. I close my eyes and clench my teeth together.

"How you holding up, man?" he questions, his voice raw with emotion. The chair at my desk squeaks with his weight.

I let out a resounding sigh. "I'm not. Chelsea breezed in here with the key I never knew she had made and told Dani about the kiddie porn."

He groans. "Yeah, I, uh, was at Andie's when she showed up bawling her fucking eyes out. Did you tell her the kiddie porn was Chelsea trying to set you up?"

Swallowing, I shake my head. "She won't talk to me. Besides, I know Dani. She's smart and wouldn't believe that bitch for a second. But she begged me not to lie to her. I told her I had no secrets and yet I harbored that one."

The chair squeaks again as he swivels. "It isn't exactly something you want to offer up," he says in my defense.

I shrug my shoulders. "She won't let me explain. I've called her no less than sixty times, Roman."

He lets out a chuckle, but it's humorless. "Chill with the stalker moves. Let her calm down. She's just really upset right now. Once she's past the initial hurt, she'll hear you out. Just give her a couple of days."

A couple of days?

I can't live without speaking to her a couple of hours. There is no way in hell I can survive days without her.

"Hmmph." That's my only response.

"Look," he grumbles. "I'll explain it to her. The whole story. If she won't listen to you, I'll get her to listen to me. Besides, I need to do some explaining myself to Andie."

I squint against the bright overhead light to look at my brother. He looks like shit. Tired. Stressed out. Lost. "What did you do?"

He scrubs his cheek with his palm. "I went off and fell into *something* for her. Like. Lust. I don't fucking know what. All I know is I like her mean ass. I like her voice when she yells at me. I like her verbal beat downs. I like her sexy round ass. And, boy, do I love her goddamned tits. But…" he trails off and scowls. "She thinks I've been just fucking around with her. Chelsea told Dani that she and I were seeing each other. Andie was pissed. It's such a clusterfuck, man."

"Wow. Andie, huh? I thought she hated you."

He laughs. "She does. That girl can hate fuck like you would not believe."

"Chelsea is like a damned hurricane. She just obliterates anything in her path. Why'd we have to be in her path?" I groan.

"Not for long," he assures me, an evil glint in his eyes. "I've been working on some stuff. Stuff I didn't want to burden you with. But things are going to get better for you and I both soon."

My phone rings and I jerk to answer it. When I see it's our sister, Reagan, calling through, I send the call to voicemail. "What am I going to do?"

He shrugs his shoulders as he stands. "Just try not to beat yourself up. If you can't get through to her, I will. Everything will work out."

His words hold a twinge of vulnerability. I know my brother. He says everything he means with confidence. And his last statement had a sliver of uncertainty.

Fuck uncertainty.

Me: Please listen.
Me: Buttercup, I love you.
Me: Hear me out. Ignoring me solves nothing.
Me: It's not what you think.
Me: Jesus Christ I fucking miss you!
Me: Dani. God. Talk to me.
Buttercup: Stop messaging. You and your cheating cocksucking whore brother can go to hell.

Andie.

Day two and Dani still won't talk to me.

Me: Tell her I love her, Andie.
Buttercup: I would tell her but that's probably a lie too.

For three days, I've stared at my ceiling. I've memorized all of the sounds of the apartment. The slow, ragged sound of my breathing. The occasional click as the heater switches on. The familiar sounds of football playing on the television as Roman watches it in the living room. I haven't moved much in three days. Mostly, I rummage around for a cup of coffee or a beer between my ceiling staring sessions. I'm not sure if I showered. I'm sure I don't care. I'm not sure if I've spoken anymore to Roman. I'm sure I don't care. I'm not sure I've done a damn thing except obsess over Dani. She's all I care about.

My door gets pushed open and for a split second, I pray it's Dani. Unfortunately, it's Roman. And fucking Reagan.

Groaning, I pull my pillow over my face. "What?"

My little sister sets her purse down on my desk and crawls into bed next to me. She yanks the pillow away and glares.

"Not again, Rammy. Get out of this bed," she orders, her pert nose flaring with her words.

I roll my eyes and start to turn over on my side. "Did he really call in reinforcements? Newsflash, sis, Dani doesn't want me anymore. This is me now. Get over it."

"Lucky for you, I'm home for Christmas break." She grabs my shoulder and yanks me back. "Nope. Not again. I remember being helpless the last time you were like this because I was halfway across the country. And the time before that, I was only fourteen and couldn't drive to save you. Well, big bro, I'm here and I can drive and I'm not going anywhere until you pull yourself out of this funk."

I flip her off.

"Told you," Roman says with a huff. "He's being a little bitch."

I flip him off too.

Reagan lets out a huff and cuddles up against me like

she used to when she was six years old. "Bub, you have to pull your shit together. You scare me when you get like this. Have you seen your face?"

Her voice sounds so small and childlike, despite the curse word, that it has me turning to regard my sister. Bright brown eyes stare at me, a mixture of fear and determination flickering in them.

"I'm fine," I lie. "Just go shopping with Mom or whatever it is you two do right before Christmas."

"You're not fine." Reagan always calls me out on my bullshit. "You have dark circles under your eyes. You have a beard almost. And you smell like Roman's dirty socks."

We both shudder. Roman used to get shit all the time from us as kids about his stinky football socks. This time it's our brother who flips us off.

"I'm fine," I try again. "If you get out of my bed, maybe I can get some sleep."

Her nose scrunches. "It's two in the afternoon. At this point, a shower and food are more important."

Closing my eyes, I ignore them both. I think about Dani. Her sweet, shy smile. Her twinkling hazel eyes. The way her laugh sounds in my ear, sending vibrations straight down to my cock.

"Come on," Roman barks out suddenly. "Reagan, let's go grab Ram some food."

My sister lets out an exasperated sigh before kissing my forehead. Then, they both quietly leave my room. I pop my eyes open again and continue my staring at the ceiling vigil. At least when I stare at the white textured surface, I don't imagine the heartbreaking look on her face.

I check my phone for the hundredth time today. Nothing.

> **Me: I think about you non-stop. I wish you would hear me out, baby. I was embarrassed. So fucking embarrassed. All I ever wanted was to be good enough for you. Man enough. Successful enough. Loving enough. Telling you about how I was fired over such a shitty thing that wasn't even my fault sickened me. I couldn't bear seeing a look of disgust in your eyes. I love you. Always. Even if you never come back to me.**

Dragging my pillow back over my head, I attempt sleep. Sleep evades me, though. Like always. The only time it doesn't evade me is when she's in my arms. When her tiny body is molded against mine and I'm free to breathe in her sweet, unique scent all night long.

Time passes. Not sure for how long. But it is dark when I finally force myself out of bed. I do stink. Badly. I manage a half-ass shower. With Dani on my mind, I jerk off under the hot spray but then give up halfway through. It doesn't mean anything getting off when the one you love isn't getting off too. After I barely towel dry my messy hair, I find a pair of grey sweatpants that hang low and loose on my hips. No underwear. No socks. No shirt. I can't be bothered by any of it.

With dragging feet, I shuffle into the kitchen. I can't remember the last time I ate anything besides a Pop-Tart. My stomach grumbles but I ignore it. I rummage in the cabinets until I find a bottle of whiskey. I unscrew the lid and take a long pull on the liquid that burns the entire way down my throat. The fire settles in the empty pit of my belly. I like how it invigorates my dying body. Dead parts reawaken.

I take my bottle back to bed with me. Sitting up against the headboard, I flip through selfies she and I took with my phone. I'm torturing myself but I can't help it. She'll always be mine even if she'll never have me again. Another long swig of whiskey.

Thirty minutes later, I'm good and drunk. I text Chelsea and tell her she's a cunt. I text Mom and tell her I'm an asshole. I text Reagan and tell her she should study psychology. I text Roman and tell him Chelsea is a cunt. I text Dani and tell her I'm an asshole. I get a text from Andie that says I'm an asshole. This goes on and on until I can't see my screen anymore. I manage to dial Dani's number in my haze.

I'm too drunk to notice if she's picked up or if it's gone to voicemail. Either way, I just talk.

"I-It's always been you, Uttercup." I groan. "Fuck. I can't think straight. You. Mine." Another groan. Another swig of whiskey. "Fuck me. I'm so goddamned sorry. She… She…that woman…Jesus!" I curse and attempt to drain my bottle. When I realize it's empty, I sling it against the wall. It thuds against it and then bounces on the carpet. "Frommm the moment you wrong texted me, I was yours," I slur. "You w-were mine, and I love you and I need you and, goddammit, please answer your phone and talk to me beautiful."

Sniffle.

I blink through my haze trying to decide if I imagined

it or not. "I can't sleep because you plague my every thought, Dannnni," I drawl out. "You're both my punishment and my reward. God fucking dammit! I'm trying to apologize and it's all coming out wrong."

Another sniffle.

She really is there.

"Baby," I groan. "Jesus, I love you. Hear me? I love you. Come back to me. I can't live without you. I'm drowning in my thoughts for you. There's no color or sound or light. Just sadness and fucking despair. I need you, baby. Don't you need me too?"

Click.

Howling out in pain that I can feel with every fiber of my being, I throw my phone. It too thuds somewhere in my room. I fist the covers and clench my eyes closed. Emotion chokes my throat. I feel as though a two-hundred-pound man is sitting on my chest. I can't breathe. Fuck. My heart is throbbing hard and painfully inside my empty chest—as if now that she's gone, it has nothing to beat for.

Please come back to me, Dani.

Chapter Seventeen

Dani

I Just Want to Sleep

"*Honey, I'm home!*" I hear Andie's voice from deep under the blankets. Her footsteps get louder and then the mattress dips with her weight. "Hey girlfriend, you get out of this bed yet today?" She tries pulling the covers off me, but I hold tight barricading myself deep inside. "I take that as a no. Well listen, I think it's great and all that you want to spend the rest of your life in my comforter igloo, but you're going to have to make some decisions here soon. Like if you want to eat or wither away, keep your job, since you've called in sick the last three days and I can only tell Harold so many times that you're a bleeding mess, or have the stomach flu, shitting all over yourself."

I grunt, throwing the covers off my face. "You did not." I blink a few times, the brightness hurting my sensitive eyes. Swollen from the nonstop crying, I lift my arm to block the light.

She smiles gently. "I didn't. Well, kinda didn't. But you know him. He's itching to make an example out of someone and since you're officially runner up on most consecutive days of calling in sick…"

At this point I couldn't care less. Let Harold stick-up-his-ass Sphincterson fire me. I hate that job anyway. I try grabbing for the covers, but this time Andie puts up a fight. "Dani, no. I love you, girl, but I can't watch you do this anymore. You're worrying me. This isn't healthy." She lets out a huff. "Not to mention, Marilyn Manson hates me. He gives me the stink-eye when I go feed him."

I try another tug, but she's not letting up. I groan, giving up and turning, offering her my back. My heart aches for my kitty, but it aches worse for Ram. "Well, I'm sick of this too. I'm sick of feeling so hurt. So lost. I'm sick of crying so hard that I make myself sick. I'm sick of feeling so alone and heartbroken 'cause I'm not sure I'll ever be able to fix what he did. I am just as sick as you are about what this has done to me, but I don't know how to change that." I don't know how it's possible to still cry, but the tears manage to slide down my cheeks. My shoulders begin to shake as Andie crawls fully into the bed, snuggling behind me. She wraps her arm around me, holding me as I cry. Again. It's been like this for the past three days. Three days which have felt like a lifetime of sadness and betrayal. Confusion on what to do.

Andie took my phone right from the beginning, fighting the battle with Ram for me. I didn't ask what he was texting and she didn't tell me. She said it was for the best.

One day into it though and my mind started to wonder what he was saying. Did he feel remorse? Was he sorry for lying? Hiding something so big from me. Was he hurting as bad as I was? Was he over it and already moving on?

I cry harder thinking about the last one. What if he just gave up? Andie assured me at one point on day two, when I was staring at my phone, that he was super active in being an annoying asshole, and I'd better hope I have an unlimited plan because he won't shut the fuck up. It was the first, small, but something, giggle I had shown in days.

"I'm sorry you're hurting, honey. I just want you to be happy. And back to the beautiful, kind, and cheery Dani I'm used to."

And so do I. But I'm afraid that I don't know how to get back there. Or if I ever can. She hugs me tighter as the sound of loud banging comes from the front door. The banging stops, then automatically starts again, this round more aggressive.

"Jesus, if that asshole had the nerve to come over here." My body tenses thinking he might be here. So close. Just outside that door. Andie disappears on a mission, and I hear the clatter of her heels slamming on the wood floor as she makes her way to the door. It's seconds after that I hear the door thrown open and the yelling begins. Afraid she's going to kill him, I jump out of bed, heading for them.

Shock, then disappointment sets in, when I see Roman with a girl standing at the threshold of her apartment.

"You douchebag, motherfucker! Coming here with one of your sluts!" Andie goes to swing at Roman, but he catches her wrist.

"Calm the fuck down, woman. She's my sister. Her name's Reagan."

Andie stares at the other woman with her mouth gaping open in shock while I scrutinize the girl next to Roman. I automatically see the similarities. Matching hair color and eyes, she also has the same nose as Ram. Just thinking his name brings back the hurt.

"Oh, well I'm sorry I called you a slut. It's your cunt of a brother who's the slu—"

With a gasp out of Andie, Roman charges for her, lifting her up and throwing her over his shoulder. "Put me down, you big oaf!"

"No. You're gonna hear me out and you're gonna stop calling me names and hitting me!"

"NEVER!" Andie yells just as Roman enters her bedroom, kicking the door closed with his heel. Ram's sister and I stare at the closed door. We hear a squeal, and I assume Roman just dropped her onto her bed.

"OUCH! You bit me!" Andie snarls.

"You just tried to rip my balls off!" Roman yells. "Fuck, you're crazy."

"You're an asshole."

It gets eerily quiet for a few seconds, until it's quiet no more.

"Oh my God, are they doing it right now?" Reagan gasps.

"Ew, I think they are." I turn to their sister and we both start laughing. "I'm sorry, how rude of me. Please come inside. We can turn on the television in hopes to drown them out."

She smiles, that Holloway smile, and follows me to

the couch. We both sit, and I turn on the television. *It's a Wonderful Life* plays on the screen.

"I'm Reagan, by the way. Roman and Ram's baby sister. Nice to officially meet you."

"Oh, you must think my manners are horrible." I stick my hand out. "I'm Dani. You're super pretty." And she is.

"Thanks, so are you. You look very sad, though. I'm sorry my brother made you so sad." I'm embarrassed that she can tell I'm suffering, but at this point, it seems impossible to hide it. My normal luster has dulled. I know I've dropped weight, even in the three short days, from lack of eating and crying.

"Me too," I reply sadly.

"You seem super nice, though!" She beams. "Not kinda loco, like your friend. No offense." I laugh because she's right. Andie *is* crazy.

Uncomfortable silence falls upon us. My chest aches with the pain only Ram can dole out to me. Breaking up with Daryl was annoying and frustrating. Losing what I had with Ram is soul crushing and killer.

"Dani," Reagan murmurs, dragging me from my inner painful thoughts. "Can I tell you a story?"

I turn to her, and nod. She smiles, looking thankful. Maybe she thought I'd have turned her down. "As I said, I'm the youngest of us three. Roman and I are eight years apart, Ram and I six. Roman and I weren't really close when I was little. He was already into his friends, school, and sports. He didn't really want to be bothered by his little sister. But Ram. He was always there for me. When I was little, at night, I would be too scared to go to my mom and dad if I wet the bed or had bad dreams. Not that they would have been mad. But I was embarrassed, so I would always go to Ram. He would clean me up or calm me. And then I would cuddle in his bed with him, listening to him tell me stories, until I fell asleep. He just took care of me. He always has. He was such a lover as a kid, and one growing up. He cared for his family, his friends, and he looked out for what was his. He kicked a boyfriend's ass once for cheating on me, left parties to come pick me up at the mall because my car would break down, and he would make sure I was doing my homework even when all I wanted to do was play video games with him. He was my best friend."

She pauses a moment to make sure I'm still following her. I'm not sure if she notices, but I'm chewing on my lower lip, trying to hide my building emotions. Hearing what a loyal brother Ram was makes me thankful Reagan has somebody like him.

"As much as Ram would mess with me, telling me I was *his* best friend, I always knew his was my dad. It wasn't his friends from the neighborhood or school. Or even Roman. It was our dad. Did you know that Ram didn't even want to go to college? He just wanted to go straight into working with my dad, learning everything from him. He said he didn't need a degree. He had my dad. As much as my dad was touched, he drilled the importance of an education and forced him to go, telling him there would always be a spot for him when he returned. He would have a degree and they could start a company together. Father and son."

I lift my hand to wipe a tear that's escaped my eye. Without even hearing the rest of this story, I know the end affects Ram in so many ways.

"My dad died during Ram's second year of college. He was diagnosed with cancer during a regular checkup. My mom and dad chose not to tell us kids, because they didn't want us to worry. They thought they would work with the doctors, hopefully do the rounds of chemo the doctor recommended without having to burden us, and move on.

My dad caught some bug. My parents had been out during a Christmas festival. My dad, the typical stubborn man he was, didn't wear a heavy enough jacket, picked up a cold. Due to the cancer, his body wasn't strong enough to fight it and he died not long after. Ram found out Dad was on his deathbed when he came home for Christmas break."

I gasp at her words, bringing my hands to my mouth trying to cover my choked sob.

"Once Ram found out Dad had been sick for some time, he went berserk. *How dare they keep something so important from us*, he'd said. How my mom was so selfish. He said some nasty things to us all. He then blamed himself for going to school. If he never went he would have been home. He could have helped in some way. He just couldn't get over he didn't get to spend more time with our dad toward the end. I don't think he has ever forgiven my mom, maybe even my dad for it."

She reaches for my hand, patting the top of it. I grab for hers, showing my remorse for her loss. She continues, "I'm sorry. I don't mean to tell you this to make you upset. That's not my point."

"I know. I'm just so sad for you all. To lose a parent. I can't imagine." Tears sneak out, despite my need to hold it together in front of her.

"Thank you. It's been a long time. The sadness never really goes away. I miss him every day, but I also know what a great dad he was when he was with us."

I nod. "I bet he was."

"My point is, that Ram has never truly loved anyone as much as he loved my dad. I know it sounds weird in a way, but they had a bond that I don't think Roman nor I ever shared. My mom either. And when he died, so did a piece of Ram. He was never truly the same. He became depressed. Gave the family tons of scares. He went off the grid and we didn't know if he was dead or alive. It took years for him to find happiness in small things. I went and saw Ram today. And the condition he's in right now, it brings back a lot of scary memories from when Dad died. That's how bad he is without you."

I begin to sob. I can't hold in the guilt or the pain. Reagan leans in, wrapping her arms around me, holding me while I cry on her shoulder.

"I know he lied. And he's a dummy for doing it. But if I can ask anything of you, please hear him out. I love my brother, and my brother loves you. It's his responsibility to explain to you why he didn't tell you everything, but I know for a fact that whatever it is she told you, it's all lies. Chelsea set my brother up. He's not what she said or accused him of being."

I pull away looking into her eyes and all I see is honesty. She continues with a hopeful smile. "Please. I'm worried about him. If I didn't know he was innocent of what that tramp is accusing him of, I wouldn't be here talking to you."

How could I have not thought about him and his depression? Just when I thought he might have moved on, he's really at home suffering. I wipe at my soaked cheeks.

"I love your brother." The words finally leaving my lips feel strange. Especially since I'm saying them to his sister and not him.

"I know you do. You wouldn't be this sad if you didn't. And he loves you something fierce. I can see it in the way he's hurting too. Go to him. Hear him out. What you two share is something extremely special."

I grab her and hug her tight. "Thank you," I whisper and pull away. I stand, knowing I need to shower first.

"Uh," she says with a groan. "I'm just going to, uh, sit here and turn the volume up while I wait for my brother. Those two seem to be getting louder in there." We both laugh just as the constant thump of the headboard banging echoes throughout the small apartment.

"Yeah. Good thinking."

It's been days since I've ventured outside, and the realization of how much snow is on the ground excites me. It takes me almost twenty minutes to get all the snow off my car. I drive carefully this time over to Ram's, making sure not to have a replay of the other day. Three stitches to the forehead is a sure way to drive safe.

I'm anxious to see Ram. I thought to call him or text, letting him know I was coming over, but then I chickened out. Despite the major issue between us, I've missed him so much. I've missed his touch, his laughter, and his small endearments. I've missed the fullness in my heart of being with him.

I make it to his place, and by the time I'm lifting my hand to knock on his door, my nerves are out of control. I realize my hand is shaking. Three knocks in and no one answers. That would just be my luck. Him not being here. I turn the knob and realize the door is unlocked. Slowly opening the door, I stick my head in.

"Ram?"

I'm met with silence, so I take another step inside their place. One quick scan shows me the place is a mess. Nothing rests on the coffee table, as it is now littering the floor. Couch cushions have been tossed, the kitchen chairs knocked over, and the tree… The Christmas tree is lying on its side, surrounded by broken ornaments. I walk in and the door closes behind me.

"Ram?" Silence. Worry sets in that something is wrong. I walk over some couch cushions making my way to Ram's room. Searching for my phone in my purse, I find it ready to call Roman.

"Ram?" I murmur as I enter his room. It's then I see him. And my heart breaks all over again. He's sitting at the end of his bed, his head hanging low. Days worth of stubble is covering his normally clean shaven face. He doesn't register my presence, and when I stand in front of him, his bloodshot eyes don't move from the object he's holding. I bring my vision to where his eyes are locked and I see it.

My ornament.

"You were going to say it. The three words I was waiting for you to say. You were going to say it, and I fucked it up." He doesn't raise his eyes to me. His focus is on the ornament, the personalized message staring back at him.

"Ram…" I say his name, needing him to acknowledge me. To show me his eyes.

"I just had to be honest with you." His voice cracks. "I would have gotten those words. I would have kept you. But I fucked it all up."

I take a step closer. He's starting to worry me. I wish he would just look at me. Kneeling down, I place my hand over the ornament to break his connection.

"Ram, look at me, please."

"So I can see disgust in your eyes? Hate? Are you here to tell me off? Make me hate myself even more than I already do?" His words are killing me. He sounds so defeated. So broken, and my heart bleeds for him. The scent of alcohol fills the room. The empty liquor bottles littering the floor tell me he's been drinking heavily.

"Ram, that's not why I'm here. I want to talk." It's then he lifts his eyes to mine. "Oh, Ram, what have you been doing to yourself?"

"I've been fucking dying."

My tears begin to fall. I bring my hands up, cupping his face. "Please talk to me."

His eyes shine with unshed tears. "I can't sleep. I can't sleep without you in my arms. I can't…" A single tear races down his bearded face.

"Ram." His name is a choked sob off my lips as I wrap my arms around him. His body quakes, his silent sobs gutting me.

"I just want to sleep," he whispers. "I want to sleep so I can dream you're still here."

"Shhh," I coo as I guide him up the bed. It's like he's on autopilot. I pull down the covers and kick off my shoes before crawling into the bed beside him. My arm wraps around his solid frame and it feels nice to be glued to his side once again.

He snuggles his face into my hair and inhales me. I feel his lips press against my head and he brings his arms around me. "Why do the people I love so much end up leaving me?" he whispers, so softly I almost don't hear it.

"I'm here. Sleep, okay? I'm here."

His breathing settles, and within minutes, I can tell he's passed out.

Sleep doesn't find me as easily, and as I lay here holding my broken man, I cry.

Chapter Eighteen

Ram

> **No Secrets.**
> **No lies.**

M Y HEAD THROBS AND I FEEL LIKE I'M GOING TO suffocate. After three days of no sleep hell, my body seems to have given up and I crashed. I groan against the light streaming in the window and try to take my other pillow to put over my eyes.

But someone is lying on it.

A painful thump in my chest reminds me my heart is still alive inside, even if just barely. I inhale a scent that makes my belly flop. Familiar. Mine. But then my chest is aching again, much like it did last night.

She's not mine.

I lost her.

I clench my eyes closed, trying to remember how beautiful she was in my dreams last night. Her brown hair was damp and had been pulled into a messy bun.

She had a tearstained face and bloodshot eyes. That's all I really remember.

She touched me.

Hugged me.

Told me it was safe to sleep.

Another painful groan from me. I sit up, fighting the churning in my stomach, and peel off my T-shirt. When I lie back down, I force myself to look on the bed beside me. To acknowledge the fact that she's not here.

Dragging my eyes over, I get another jostling jolt to the heart. Dani lies there, looking so small and perfect, still fully clothed.

It wasn't a dream.

Unless I'm still drunk.

Her waking moan acts like an alarm to my dick. I lie down beside her and stroke her hair. She feels real. When she rolls over and peers up at me with her sleepy hazel eyes, I know it's not a dream. I simply drank myself to death and I'm in heaven.

"Oh, Ram," she whispers, her delicate hand gently touching my scruffy cheek. "What happened to us?"

I clench my jaw and swallow. Emotion claws at my chest, but I keep it at bay. "I broke us."

Her dark brows furrow together and she shakes her head. She slides her palm to my neck before touching my upper bare chest. "I missed you. Apparently, I can't function without you." She lets out a laugh, but it comes with tears.

I tentatively reach for her. When she doesn't jerk away, I swipe away her tears. "I can't function without you either," I grunt. "What happened to your forehead?"

She scrunches her nose and rolls her eyes. "Snow happened. I had a teensie weensie little accident."

I jerk up and glare at her. "What? Where? When? How?"

A sweet smile tugs at her lips as she urges me to lie back down. "Yep, an accident. Outside of this building in my car. The day I ran from you. I was too upset and tried to go too fast."

A growl rumbles from me. I barely manage to hiss out any words. "This is all my fault."

She strokes her fingers through my messy hair. "This isn't all your fault. You didn't make me drive like an idiot. That was all me. Besides, I'm fine now. Everything is fine. Well…" she smirks. "Not my job. That's certainly not fine, but I don't really like it there anyway."

"Baby…"

She winces at the endearment and my heart shuts down. How do I fucking fix us?

"I," I start, and then cough away the hoarseness in my throat. "I should have told you how I was fired. I should have explained everything. Hell, I wanted to. Badly. But I was just so fucking mortified you would think less of me."

I finally allow my hand to touch her. I'm dying to caress her and hold her. My palm splays out on her hip before drawing her closer to me.

"Ram," she says with a sigh. "Why would I think less of you for something that's untrue? I know you. You're a good man. Something clearly happened, but I don't believe for one second that those allegations were true."

Letting out a huff of air, I shake my head. "Of course they weren't true. It's all so stupid. I'd been seeing Chelsea for several months. I thought things were getting serious despite knowing better. Chelsea is known for liking shiny toys. To her, I was a shiny toy. When I wasn't so shiny anymore and boring, she wanted to get rid of me. But it's not her style to simply breakup with someone."

Dani's eyes narrow at me and I can tell she's angry. I keep talking before I lose my nerve.

"Anyway, since I worked for her dad's company that she also worked for, the simple breakup would have left me still there and in her way. So Chelsea decided to make a big production. She sent me something. A link. I'd opened it not understanding exactly what it was. As soon as I realized it was something awful, I pushed off the power on my computer. It was too late. The IT department had been notified. They came in with disgust in their eyes and the owner on their heels. Once they deduced that there was child porn on my computer, old man Tucker told my brother to get rid of me. Roman fired me on the spot. In front of Chelsea and everyone. I could tell it tore up my brother, having to do it without getting to the bottom of what happened." I close my eyes and sigh. "Anyway, that's what happened." When I reopen my eyes, Dani's nostrils are flaring.

"That bitch," she hisses.

One side of my mouth quirks up in a half-smile. It disarms her for a minute because she smiles too.

"I missed that smile," she tells me, her cheeks turning a pretty pink color. "Why didn't you tell them what really happened, Ram?"

I swallow and shrug. "I wanted to give Chelsea the benefit of the doubt. That either it was a mistake or that she'd stick up for me to her father. Neither of those scenarios were the case. She moved on to Blake in accounting."

"And then Roman in marketing," she bites out, fury blazing in her eyes.

"Roman wouldn't touch her. He hates her," I tell her firmly.

She bites on her bottom lip. "No secrets? No lies?"

Nodding, I give her a frown. "No secrets. No lies."

"She told me she was seeing Roman."

I laugh and it's bitter. "Yeah fucking right. She's a liar."

"Oh, I can see that now. I sort of told Andie, though. And for two people who 'aren't seeing each other,' she really got pissed." But then she smiles broadly. "He must have gotten through to her, though, because I left them as they worked together to drive the headboard through the wall. Your poor sister."

My eyes widen. "You met Reagan?"

She blushes and nods. "She looks a lot like you. I like her. Let's just say she made me see things differently."

I spear my fingers into her hair, no longer able to keep my distance. My lips brush against hers for a brief moment before she pushes me away.

"Wait…"

Pain slices through my heart. I'd assumed wrong. She won't be able to forget so easily. "I really am sorry, baby. I should never have kept that from you."

She chuckles. "The past is behind us. We're moving forward now. You and I operate better as two parts of one amazing whole. Now that I've got you back, we can move forward like we should have a lot sooner. And for that, *I'm* sorry."

I frown and shake my head. "You have *nothing* to apologize for."

Her thumb shushes me. "Actually, I lied too."

My heart rate quickens.

"I lied to myself and I lied to you by omission. Ramsey Holloway, I love you. I should have told you some time ago. Especially on the many occasions you told me. Because it's true. I do love you. I think I've loved you from the moment you called me Buttercup."

I beam at her. "Then I love you too, Buttercup." All the pain that had been threatening to consume me fades away like a sad song that's ending. Now, a new beat begins to play in my heart. Something hopeful and upbeat. Something ours.

"Now will you kiss me?"

She nods and lets me pull her to me. Our lips meet, almost shyly at first. But then the slow, aching hunger within each of us begins to claw its way out. Moans escape and our kisses become more fervent. Tongues fight for purchase in each other's mouths. Lips suck and teeth bite. I don't even realize I'd been tugging at her sweater until it's off her head and sailing off the bed. My palm finds her tit through her bra. Round and full and mine. I nudge her onto her back before I begin trailing kisses from the corner of her mouth, along her slender neck, across her collar bone, and then to her cleavage. She lets out a whine when I bite her flesh through her bra.

"More, Ram," she murmurs, her fingers tugging at my hair.

I slide my hand beneath her and unhook her bra in one fluid motion. And in the next, that delicate piece of clothing is sailing through the air. Next her leggings and panties are gone. I leave her socks on so her little toes don't freeze. My mouth craves to kiss her everywhere. But when I spend a little too much time worshipping her entire body, including her knees and shins, she lets out an exasperated huff.

"So help me if you don't slip off those sweatpants and push inside of me in the next three seconds, I'm walking right out that door."

I start to laugh because her face is all business. Needy and desperate.

"As you wish," I tell her with a wink. I shove my sweatpants down my thighs and push her knees apart. "Say it again." Leaning forward, I hover over her tiny body letting my thick, engorged cock rest heavily on her cunt. "Please. Say it."

"It."

I growl at her and nip at her bottom lip. "Such a smartass."

She giggles until I drive my cock into her wet entrance in one hard thrust. "OMIGOD!"

"You're mine forever, Buttercup," I tell her, our mouths soft and wet against each other.

"Yours," she agrees. "Yes."

"Say it."

She giggles but indulges me. "I love you, my sweet, sexy man."

I devour her mouth and buck into her like a wild animal. Her body shudders, always so sensitive to how we mold together. When she cries out and her cunt grips my dick, I let out a pleased groan before my release surges from me almost painfully. I collapse on her small body and nuzzle my nose against her ear. "Don't ever leave me again." My pleaded words are barely a whisper but she hears me.

"Never again."

"Wow, that was fun. Not." Andie blows a blonde hair from her forehead and attempts to ignore Roman. He's kind of hard to ignore, though, my brother. Giant and imposing and all up in her personal space. They're still in denial. As if we'll all make fun of them for seeing each other. It isn't as if we can't hear them fuck every ten minutes in whatever room is closest.

"Thank you," Dani tells her. "The tree looks much better upright." She shoots me a sad stare. I'd kind of lost my fucking head while drunk last night and destroyed the living room. Thankfully, everyone loves me and worked together to help clean it up. The only ornament that wasn't broken was the one Dani made for me, which now hangs proudly at my eye level.

"You're looking lots better," Reagan says with a grin. "It's a good thing, too. Tomorrow's Christmas Eve and Mom would be pissed if you showed up being Grumpy Gus."

I ruffle her hair and she swats at me.

"So now what?" my sister questions as she picks a piece of lint off Dani's sweater. I don't miss the way they giggle at each other's quiet jokes. It warms me to know they get along so well already.

"We get that bitch back," Andie practically growls.

I raise an eyebrow in question. "Chelsea?"

"I like to refer to her as Fake Bitch Cunt, but whatever," Andie huffs. "This is still happening, right Oaf?" Her eyes dart over to my brother, who rolls his eyes.

"Must you call me that?" he grumbles. "But yeah."

I blink at him stupidly. "What do you mean? We're getting her back? How?"

Dani's arms wrap around my middle and she leans her head on my chest. "She hurt you. She tried to hurt us. It's time she learns she can't mess with people's lives like that." Her fingers clutch onto the front of my shirt and she lifts her gaze to mine as if to make sure what she said is okay.

"Okay, I'm listening. But isn't it better to just ignore her? She'll go away eventually," I tell them with a groan.

"Until Fake Bitch Cunt comes back trying to stir up more shit," Andie explains with over-exaggerated hand gestures. "FBC *will* be back. Probably to be the one to object right in the middle of your wedding ceremony!"

Dani tenses and I hug her tighter. She's probably embarrassed that her friend assumed we would get married one day. Her friend is right. And just as soon as we get past Christmas, I'm taking my beautiful Buttercup and I'm going to buy her a ring.

"She's right," Roman groans, as if he hates even agreeing with her. She flashes me a triumphant smile. "Chelsea has gotten three employees just this month fired for various things. These were good, solid employees. It's ridiculous. I'd been attempting to concoct something to get her back when I'd just had enough. I quit on Friday."

"You *what*?" I bark out.

His dark eyes bore into mine and he nods his head.

224

"She forced me to fire my little brother. From that second on, I was never loyal to that company. I've been working on a plan ever since."

"What's the plan?" I demand. My chest swells, though, that my brother hates them just as much as I do.

"James Tucker is getting ready to retire," Roman explains. "It was always assumed he'd just hand over the reins to Chelsea. But James is old school. He's a good guy despite the bitch he raised. I've been talking to him about selling Tucker Advertising to me."

I blink at my brother. "You can't afford that."

He shakes his head. "If *we* touch the money Dad left us," he says and gestures to himself, then me, and then Reagan. "*We* could afford to do that."

Reagan grins. "I'm in."

Dani squeezes me in a supportive way that has my heart rate slowing. "Okay…" I utter, still not convinced this is the best plan.

"But, he won't sell unless there is absolutely no way he can trust Chelsea to effectively run the company once he steps away. Some of those clients he's been building relationships with since the seventies, long before she was born. It'll kill him to hand them over to her if she's not serious about her role," he tells me. "So…"

Andie cuts him off and pats his solid chest. "We're going to bring the bitch down."

Dani and Reagan laugh.

"I'm game for making her pay for ruining my life… twice…but…how?" I question.

A wicked grin turns Andie's lips up on both corners. "Roman's going to get her to Bender's. Brett and I are going to do the rest." She winks at me—a wink that says, *don't worry, man, I've got this.*

"What do *I* do?"

Dani looks up at me and grins. "You just have to show up with me."

"And what are *we* going to do?" I ask with a smirk. She's so damn cute when she's being devious. When I'd told her, after the second round of make-up sex, that Chelsea had stripped down in my room in an attempt to seduce me, I thought I was going to have to tie Dani to the bed to keep her from going after her. But... *No secrets. No lies.* I am as transparent as a fucking ghost now as far as my girlfriend is concerned.

"Well," Andie tells me. "After FBC gets good and drunk, she's going to admit that she set you up because she's a duplicitous cunt. *Then...*"

Roman lets out a growl. "*Then* we finish the job. I'll meet with James and show him exactly *why* his daughter is unfit to run Tucker Advertising. And then we're going to buy that company right out from under her feet."

I squeeze my girl against me. "Let's get this show on the road."

Chapter Nineteen

Andie

> ### It's Show Time

"**A**ND WHY AGAIN ARE YOU DRESSED LIKE THAT?" Brett asks, his fucking eyes glued to my tits.

"Because I need to connect with the super cunt so she talks to me and confesses that she's a cunt and got our boy fired." I don't think he even registers what I said. "For fuck's sake my eyes are up here." He blinks. Up they go. Back to reality.

"Shit, darlin', you gotta nice rack. Maybe some time, you and I should—"

My phone dings, cutting off whatever he was going to say.

Roman: She's going to be there in two minutes. Don't fuck this up. And pull your shirt up for Christ's sake.

Me: Go fuck yourself. Probably gonna let

> **Brett fuck these to thank him for the good job he'll do tonight.**
>
> **Roman: WTF? He better not fucking touch you.**
>
> **Me: Not your call, asswipe. Now, I'm definitely letting him see the goods. See how you like that… <middle finger emoji>**

"Okay, she's about to walk in. Get ready." I lift my hand and do my secret signal, so Dani and Ram, who are hiding in a booth in the corner, know it's almost show time. I take a sip of my drink, watching the door from the corner of my eye. Like clockwork, it opens and a woman fitting the description of the one and only FBC walks in.

"Well, she certainly looks like she knows her way around a dick," Brett says, wiping his hands on his bar towel then swings it over his shoulder. I fight not to look, but I catch her in my peripheral view. Sadly, I can see the appeal. She's tall, beautiful, and definitely has a whore mouth.

"Stick to the plan or I swear, I'll cut your dick off."

He grunts, most likely the image of him dick-less a scary thing. He grabs for his potential victimized dick. "Fuck, you freak the hell out of me."

"Good. Now get ready. It's show time." Just then, like fucking magic, she sits down next to me. We roped in Sylvia to make sure the rest of the bar stools were full.

"Hey, handsome. I'll take an appletini," FBC orders, placing her Louis Vuitton purse on the bar. *Damn I want that purse.* Her eyes search the bar, probably for Roman. She glances quickly at me and smiles. After a moment, she grabs her phone from her purse checking to see if she has a text. Per our plan, she will. Roman will text her telling her he's running late.

"Here you go, darlin'. Why is a beautiful woman like yourself drinking alone tonight?" Brett questions, laying the bait. Her dick-sucking smile perks at Brett. But mine would too. Brett is super-hot. And let's be honest, if I didn't have my hands full with my own fucking dumb ape, I would try and hit that shit too.

"Oh, aren't you sweet. I'm waiting for someone. Running late, go figure. But you're more than welcome to keep me company while I wait." She grins again. I fight not to shove that amazing purse down her throat and tell her cunt ass to stay the fuck away from my—*Ew!* What the hell was I just going to say!? I shake off the insanity and turn to my target.

"Men, fuck 'em. Always late. Never know how to really treat us ladies." I smile confidently and take a sip of my Sprite. The not drinking part wasn't my idea. Mostly Dani and fuckhead Roman. Something about how they're afraid I might 'ruin our plan if I drank and let my mouth run.' No faith in me.

"Girl, you have no idea. It's hard to find a good man anymore. But I snatched me one up now." She grins seductively, sipping down her frilly drink. My hand itches to reach up and choke her, but I maintain my composure.

"I *so* get it." I wave to Brett, lifting my drink. "Excuse me, I'll have what she's having. Looks way too tasty not to try." Brett gapes at me, knowing drinking was not part of the plan. He was instructed *not* to feed me booze, and not if but when I ordered. We all knew it was only a matter of time.

"Are you sure…"

"As sure as it would suck to be dick-less."

His eyes widen, his hand covering his dick.

"And get my new friend here a refill while you're at it," I bark out. "On me."

"You got it," he grumbles before stalking off to make our drinks.

"Thanks," she says, her light brown eyes twinkling. "They really make you all warm inside. Trust me. I love putting a few of these down." Her eyes narrow and she leans in to whisper, "Gets me horny." Then, she giggles, admitting what a filthy cunt she is. I mimic her laughter and stick my hand out.

"Hi, I'm Andrea."

FBC returns the gesture, her nails perfectly manicured and a charm bracelet dangling off her wrist. *What the fuck is this bitch like five?* "Hi, Chelsea. Nice to meet you. Love the outfit, by the way. Super my style." Bingo.

I flash her a smile and wave at my chest. "You can never go wrong with showing a little cleavage. I do it all the time at work. Really reels in the guys." I give her a conspiratorial wink. "Man, I just got one earlier this week. Kinda tricked him, though," I say, leaning closer so I can whisper. "Told him my manager wanted to see him. Got him in the supply closet. Let him suck on these for a bit," I say, lifting up my tits crudely. "And then when I was done getting my fill, told him I recorded it, and suggested taking this horrid project off my hands or else I would tell everyone." I giggle profusely. Maybe a little too much. I wait for her to take the second line of bait.

And she does.

Her eyes light up. Like she just met her new best friend. *Too bad bitch, Dani has that job.* "No way! That's perfect!" she exclaims and claps her hands together. "So what happened?"

Brett puts our fresh drinks on the bar and rolls his eyes at me before stepping away again.

"Oh," I explain, "he completed the project for me all right. Did a wonderful job, and guess what? I got a raise!" I grin, and lift my drink. She actually cheers me. The urge to smash my martini glass into hers is overwhelming.

"Girl, I think you and I just may have become best friends! I *love* your style." She takes a hefty sip, finishing off her martini. Grabbing for the fresh one and taking a sip off the top, she says, "Well I can top that." *BINGO.* This bitch is practically deep throating my bait.

"There was this jerk at work. Totally blew me off. Said he had a girlfriend or whatnot. So *I* took this dirty picture of myself. Then while he went to the bathroom, I uploaded it to his phone, making it look like he took it. Told him, I was going to threaten to tell my daddy what a perv he was, and he wouldn't have to worry about his girlfriend anymore. He quit the next day! No one turns *me* down." Her eyes are calculating and evil.

I cover my mouth, eyes wide. I laugh, pretending she's so awesome and clever, but mentally, I'm kicking her in her stupid cunt. "Oh girl! You're awesome! I wish I would have thought of that. I had a guy like that once. Told me he wasn't interested in me so, I went girl cray. I stole his phone while he was in a meeting and took scandalous pics of myself. *Then* sent them to my boss with a message that said, 'Look what I'm going to hit later.' Of course, since my boss is *my* daddy too," I lie. "Jim was fired immediately. Teach him a lesson in letting a good thing slip away."

We both laugh and raise our glasses in another toast. Taking two hefty gulps, I wave for Brett to refill us. He looks at me quizzically and I give him the *off with your head* look. And he knows *exactly* which head I'm referring to.

"Wow, we are drinking these fast. By the time my date gets here, I'm already going to be ready for him to take me back to his place." Her giggly comment is like nails on a chalkboard for me. I'm squeezing my glass so tight I'm surprised it doesn't shatter in my hands.

"Oh, yay. Drunk sex is the best isn't it? I just love getting fucked royally by random men. I don't bother with relationships. No one is good enough for this prized possession," I say, taking my finger and pointing to myself. She nods in agreement and takes another drink.

"Agreed, girl. I swear," she complains. "All men I've dealt with lately have been total pussies. I'm not even sure this one is going to cut it, but we shall see. He's rich and from what I hear has a nice cock. Love the ones that look large in the cock region, ya know?"

Rage consumes me because for some odd reason, I don't like her thinking about Roman's cock whatsoever. I'm going to gut her. Fuck this plan. That's it. I'm going AWOL and fucking this bitch up—

"Two fresh martinis for the hottest chicks in this bar," Brett interrupts my internal fury. "But you, sweetheart," he points to Chelsea and gives her a smoldering stare, "look like you could use some extra attention."

I narrow my eyes at him, wondering what the fuck he's

doing. This is *not* part of the plan. But neither is me drinking and planning to kill our target with my bare hands.

"I like attention," Chelsea purrs. "What exactly did you have in mind?" Using the underside of her finger, she runs it along the top of her martini glass, a suggestive smile playing at her lips.

"Why don't I show you the back room?" he questions, his voice low as he leans across the bar, blatantly staring at her tits. "It's pretty huge." And then he smirks as if his words have double meaning.

What the fuck!?

Chelsea receives a text message, which I know will be Roman telling her he is going to be running another thirty minutes late. She lets out an annoyed huff, but then brings her sleazy eyes back to Brett.

"Well I *do* have some time to kill," she says and then stands. She's a little wobbly since by now we are on our third martini in only a short amount of time. Brett walks from out behind the bar, taking Chelsea's hand.

"Watch my purse, kay?" She winks at me and then they're gone.

"What the FUCK!?" My phone goes off instantly.

Dani: What just happened?

Me: Dude…the bitch is pretty surely going to suck some cock.

Roman: How's it going?

Me: Fuck yourself.

Dani: Oh my God! While she's waiting for Roman!? <wide-eyed emoji>

Me: For real. She's a real treat.

Roman: Ram just told me you were

drinking! WTF! I thought we said no booze?

Me: I hate you.

Dani: Roman keeps firing off texts to Ram. He knows you're drinking <oops face emoji> He's pissed.

Me: Roman can choke on his own dick.

Roman: You don't hate me and you know it.

Dani: Ram just told Roman that Chelsea went to the back with Brett.

Me: Good. Hope it hurts his pretty little cocksucking feelings.

Dani: <shocked emoji>

Roman: What's happening?

Me: Your girlfriend is sucking off Brett. Gonna go back there next.

My phone rings instantly, Roman's call coming through. I click ignore, just as Brett and Chelsea come strolling in from the back. Brett is smiling and Chelsea looks just as cunty as she did before.

"I'm going to use the ladies' room. Be back." She waves at me and saunters off to the restroom. I worry she might see Dani and Ram at the booth on her way, but she's swaying so I'm sure she's too drunk *and* dumb to look around.

"What the fuck, dude! Getting your dick wet was not part of the plan!" I snap at Brett. He shrugs his shoulders, throwing his damn bar towel over his shoulder.

"Yeah, but you looked kind of murderous, so I had to create a diversion," he tells me with a mischievous grin.

I roll my eyes at him while finishing off my drink.

"Another one. Now. And fill hers up too. Pretty sure she can use another drink to wash down the cum dripping down her throat."

We both actually laugh at that because it's fucking funny. Finally, the bitch returns.

"Well, *that* was fun." She winks at Brett as she takes a sip of her new drink. She leans in trying to whisper, but the alcohol is affecting her senses so she says it loud enough for Mars to hear. "Great cock. I'd recommend giving it a try sometime." I hear Brett chuckle while I try to keep my jaw from falling off. This chick is a real piece of work.

"Oh, I bet," I tell her, quickly recovering and remembering my role here. "Been wanting to hit that for months. Maybe I'll try once you take off with your date." I lift my drink, insinuating her to follow. "Let's make a toast. To awesome chicks who don't take shit from anyone!" She clinks her glass with me and we both drink. I continue, "I'm loving our stories. Tell me another one!"

She puts her glass down, slapping her hands together. "So get this," she begins, her voice slurring. "This guy I was sort of into from work got boring for me. But he wouldn't be so easy to blow off since we would still have to see each other every day. To fix that little problem, I sent him a virus." She leans closer and shouts, "Kiddie porn!" Her laughter nearly has her falling off her barstool as if she just told me the world's funniest joke. "Any who. Daddy wasn't happy and made his own brother fire him. It was amazing. To watch the guy's poor face crumple. He was like a sad puppy when he was let go. How humiliating," she ends, looking satisfied with herself.

I, on the other hand, am seeing fifty shades of red. I'm fucking furious. I know the plan was to get her nice and drunk until she spilled the beans, then walk away, but there is no way that's happening. Because I *am* kinda crazy and this bitch just hit the ignition button on my crazy train. I gulp the remaining liquid in my drink and slam it down. It startles Chelsea and she jumps a bit off her seat.

"Dang girl, a little rough with that—"

I'm done listening to her skank ass. With a screech, I tackle her right off the barstool.

And the bar erupts in chaos.

We both crash to the ground with a painful thud. Chelsea squeals in surprise as I lift my closed fist and bring it smashing down on her over-botoxed face. I raise my hand for the second shot, when someone behind me rips me off her.

"Let me go! I'm going to cut this bitch!" I yell at who-ever's holding me. I'm kicking and screaming trying to get free when I catch a whiff of the familiar scent of one big 'ol asshole I know real well.

"Fucking calm down, woman!"

"No! Fuck you! I'm going to kill her!"

Chelsea is trying to stand, tenderly touching her now bleeding nose. "You crazy bitch! You hit me!"

"Yeah and I'm gonna fuck you up a whole lot more you cunt whore, fucking sleazy bitch!" I try elbowing Roman in the chest, and get a good shot because I hear him grunt. He pulls me farther away knowing with my impressive arm length, I can probably still knock her out. I see Dani and Ram run up, Ram now towering over Chelsea.

"What the f-f-fuck are *you* doing here?" she slurs, grabbing for a napkin to stop the bleeding.

"Clearing my name," he snaps. "Which you seem to have done."

Her brows raise, looking from me, back to Ram. "Well you can't prove anything. What? You think this twat's words matter? They had proof on your computer, Ramsey."

I go nuts again, kicking Roman, getting a good shot in the leg. He accidentally twitches, letting me go. I run at her, but get caught by Brett.

"You're dead bitch!" I scream and Brett, trying not to get his balls hit by my kicking feet, hands me back to Roman. "Fuck you! Let me go! I'm going to kill her!"

"This isn't your fight, woman," Roman growls against my ear. "Calm down. This is exactly why we all said you shouldn't drink."

"Fuck—"

Roman twists me in his arms. His handsome face glowers at me for a brief moment before he crushes his lips to mine. I hate the way his lips feel on mine. Soft and sexy and delicious. His breath is always minty and mixed with a hint of coffee. His tongue, as it takes no prisoners, shoves into my mouth and tastes me, fucking turning me to mush. I kiss him back just as furiously. He makes me angry most of the time, but I enjoy his kisses all of the time.

"Oh my God, Roman! What the fuck?" Chelsea bellows from behind us. I pull away, ready to go off when Dani steps in front of me.

"Remember me? I'm sure you do. Because I'm

someone you will never be. I'm Ram's girlfriend. The one he loves, and will be something more than you will ever be to anyone. Being hateful is a sad quality to have. And no matter how beautiful you may appear on the outside. It makes you ugly inside *and* out. I hope you get what you deserve. Because what you did? It's unforgivable."

Chelsea lets off an evil laugh and speaks, "You're a joke. Meek little girl who thinks she has it all. Honey, someone like you won't find love. He will get tired of you. I mean look at you. Leggings? Really? No one will believe a little runt like you—"

Ram steps next to Dani, bringing her to his chest. If I'm seeing correctly, Ram looks like he just might take a swing at her as well, which I will be jealous 'cause that bitch is mine.

"You better watch how you talk to my future wife," Ram says and everyone gasps. Including Dani. He places a kiss to the top of her head, turning his attention back to Chelsea. "And you know who your father will believe?" He holds up a cell phone. "This recording that has your confession to not only what you did to me, but to three other employees at Tucker. You're finished. Once your father gets wind of this, I doubt you will be seeing the inside of Tucker Advertising ever again."

She goes to slap Ram, but the craziest thing happens.

Dani steps forward and smacks her first. Another round of shocked gasps fill the bar, and this time, I bust out laughing. I'm laughing so hard, I buckle over in Roman's arms, tears starting to run down my face. Slow to follow, I hear Roman, then Ram joining me. It's then I hear the soft, cute chuckle of my bestie as she joins in.

She turns to look at me, her eyes filled with gleaming satisfaction, and says, "Wow, I get why you do that a lot. Very fulfilling."

At that, everyone in the bar starts laughing.

Minus Chelsea.

Chapter Twenty

Ram

Mind Blowing, Explosive, Slap Your Momma Kind Of Sex

"**D**UDE, LIGHTEN UP," I TELL MY BROTHER AS I hand him a beer. "She's probably on the rag or some shit."

Roman scrubs at his cheek and shakes his head. "Mom said," his voice gets higher to mimic our mother, '*If you like her, invite her to Christmas.*'"

"I don't talk like that!" Mom hollers from the kitchen. Reagan and Dani, who are in there with her, start giggling.

We both laugh because that woman hears everything.

"Anyway, so I invite her because I'm really fucking trying here. You know what she says to me?" Roman growls.

"Something along the lines of fuck you or fuck off or go fuck yourself?" I quip with a smirk.

He nods. "All of the above. What the hell, man? But

then she sends me this." He opens his phone and holds it up to me.

Goddamn Those Tits: What are you doing after your boring family shit?

I lift an eyebrow at him. "Goddamn Those Tits?"

A wolfish grin spreads across his face. "I mean...for real, though. Have you seen—"

I cut him off, waving at him. "First of all, try putting her actual name in your phone. I'm all for nicknames, but that's just wrong. Second of all," I utter, leaning in. "Have you tried taking her on a date or something? Your relationship is based purely on sex."

He snorts. "Mind blowing, explosive, slap your momma kind of sex," he tells me.

"I heard that," Mom hollers.

I shake my head at him. "Tell her Dani wants her to come. Play the BFF card."

He frowns as if I'm stupid, but fires off a text to her. Three seconds later, she responds. Another growl from my brother before he shows it to me.

Goddamn Those Tits: All I heard was blah, blah, blah. Are you going to lick my pussy or not?

I know Andie's crude, but damn. "Holy shit."

Roman grunts and nods. "Now you know what I'm dealing with. How the fuck am I supposed to tell her no? Furthermore, how am I supposed to go from booty call to dating? Is that even possible?"

"I don't know," I tell him honestly. "Maybe go have the mind blowing, explosive, slap your momma kind of sex and then afterward, talk to her."

He scoffs and shakes his head as if I've said something stupid. "Andie doesn't talk after sex. She throws my clothes at me and literally kicks my ass out her door. If I want a kiss, I have to endure a kick to the balls while I steal one. She's fucking impossible."

"Yet you're still trying to do the impossible," I tell him with a chuckle. "True Roman Holloway style."

"This isn't football or college or my career," he grunts. "This is Andie. She's in a whole other world of unattainable and impossible. Sometimes, I wonder if she's even worth it." But even as he says the words, I don't believe he wonders that last bit even a little.

Dani plops down on the couch beside me. "She's worth it," she tells him simply. "Andie is like a cactus. You just have to get past the prickly spurs to find her sweet center."

"Oh, I know about her sweet center," Roman murmurs.

Dani huffs and I laugh. "And what do we call that, Buttercup?"

She growls. "I'm not saying your stupid word."

"But we had a deal," I say, waggling my eyebrows at her.

"Bye," she grumbles and leaves me to go back to the women in the kitchen.

I'm still chuckling when Roman gets in a texting war with who I assume is Andie. He keeps cursing under his breath until he finally storms out of Mom's living room. It's weird. I used to hate Christmas time because it's when we lost Dad. But now that I have Dani, I like it again. She makes it fun and warm and loving. Mom and my siblings seem happy and that makes me happy. Dad would have loved Dani.

A smile ghosts my lips as my phone buzzes.

> Buttercup: I cunt believe you're making me do this.

I snort out a laugh that in turn causes a loud huff from Dani in the kitchen.

> Me: I feel like this is cheating but baby steps I suppose. This cuntversation was inevitable, you know.
> Buttercup: Cunt is the lamest word this cuntry ever came up with.
> Me: Our cuntry? I was for sure it was a British word or some shit.
> Buttercup: Only Americunts would come up with something that vulgar.
> Me: You're an Americunt.
> Buttercup: Your mom is an Americunt.
> Buttercup: OMG. I'm just kidding. Virginia is perfect. I cunt believe you just lured me into a 'your mom' joke.
> Me: LOL!! You cunt blame me for your dirty cuntversationalist ways…
> Buttercup: Cunt we move on from this already?
> Me: I'm sorry but I cunt hear you. Perhaps you should come here and sit in my lap. I have something you should cuntsider putting in your mouth.
> Buttercup: You're uncuntrollable!
> Me: I cunt control my mouth around you.

Buttercup: Speaking of mouths, my fellow Americunt, I believe I have won and you owe me something.

Me: What's that, Buttercunt?

Buttercup: Don't ever call me Buttercunt again or you'll be a single Americunt.

Buttercup: I'm waiting in your old bedroom. I cunt believe there are still posters hanging up in here from the nineties.

Me: Cunt think of a better era...

I bolt from the couch and sneak up the stairs to where my girl is waiting. A promise is a promise. A deal is a deal.

Buttercup: I cunt wait any longer...my fingers have to keep me company until that dirty mouth shows up.

A growl rumbles through my chest as I prowl down the hallway toward my door that stands ajar. When I slip inside, my sweet, beautiful girl is doing just as she says. Her hands move under the sheet and a devious smile paints her lips.

"I cunt believe you started without me," I say with a grin as I yank off my sweater and kick the door shut.

"My cunt was needy," she murmurs, a pout on her pretty plump lips.

I groan and close my eyes for a brief moment as I strip out of the rest of my clothes. When I reopen them, she's grinning at me like the cat that ate the canary. But she's got it all wrong...this weird ass bird is about to eat that pussy.

"Show me how wet our cuntversation made you," I order as I drag the sheet down her legs, baring her to me.

She's naked and squirmy and flushed and mine.

Her knees fall apart and her sweet center indeed glistens with her arousal.

"Perfect," I praise.

She lets out a low moan of appreciation when I lick her seam and then circle her clit.

"Oh my Godddddd!"

"All you had to do was say the magical word and this was all yours," I breathe against her soft flesh.

She moans and clutches my hair. "Cunt! Cunt! Cunt! Now don't stop!"

With the hunger of a hundred starved men, I feast upon her. As I suck, lick, tongue fuck her into submission, I can't help but grin. I was going to eat this pussy anyway.

"As you wish, Buttercup."

"The ham is getting cold," Mom chides, but I don't miss the pleased grin on her face. She loves Dani and seems to adore the fact that we're a serious couple.

Dani's cheeks turn bright red and she hides her face behind a curtain of her hair as she pretends to decide on a slice of ham. I simply shrug my shoulders. "Dani can get it hot again if it isn't to her liking."

She lets out a choked sound and Roman laughs from the dinner table.

"Anyway," Reagan chirps, rescuing Dani. "I have a big announcement."

We all turn to regard my little sister. She's all grown up and it makes my heart swell.

"I know I told you all I was home for break," she says

softly, a look of embarrassment on her face. "But I'm actually home for good."

Mom frowns. "But what about school?"

Reagan chews on her bottom lip and a look of guilt passes over her features. "Weren't you wondering what was taking me so long to graduate from college?"

I glance at Roman and his eyes are narrowed at her.

"We just thought you were struggling with the class load," he tells her.

Reagan shakes her head. "I graduated two years ago."

My eyes widen and Mom gasps. Dani walks up behind her and places her hands on Reagan's shoulders in a supportive gesture. She leans forward and whispers, "It's okay."

Reagan's eyes well with tears and she nods. "I'd sort of fallen for a guy I went to college with. I just…stayed…for him. That is…"

Roman growls. Mom is still in shock, just gaping at our sister.

"What happened?" I ask her softly.

"I caught him with one of my friends. It was ugly. They'd been sleeping together behind my back for a while. I don't know why I stayed for him or why I lied and told you all I was still in school. I guess I just wanted to see where it went first before I involved you all. Now, I'm glad I didn't because—"

"His ass would be dead right now," I bite out.

She flashes me an appreciative little sister smile. "Yeah. That."

"So what does this mean?" Mom questions, her voice shaking. "Is my baby girl coming back home?"

Reagan nods and glances over at Roman. "I am. I was hoping maybe that Roman would give me a job at Tucker."

Roman clenches his jaw. "No, I won't give you a job at Tucker."

Dani gasps. "But she's your sis—"

"But, as part owner, she can take whatever job she wants at Holloway Advertising and Branding," he finishes with a shit-eating grin.

Everyone lets out a collective sigh and I tug my sister from her seat up into my arms. She hugs me back as a small sob of relief escapes her. If I ever see that motherfucker who hurt her, I'll knock his front teeth in. Nobody hurts my sister.

"This calls for a celebration," Mom cheers. "Your daddy would be so proud of all three of you."

My eyes meet Dani's and hers shimmer with tears. I mouth to her that I love her. Her bottom lip quivers, but she returns the sentiment. God, I'll never get tired of that.

Reagan sniffles and makes her way around the kitchen hugging everyone, including Dani. Once Mom starts opening a bottle of wine, I steal my adorable future wife and drag her away. We pass by the bay window in the living room and it appears that more snow is falling.

"Where are we going?" she questions.

I stop in front of the tree to retrieve the small jewelry box. I was going to wait until after Christmas but when it comes to Dani, I don't want to wait another minute. When I stand, her eyes widen in surprise. "It doesn't matter where we're going," I tell her with a crooked grin. "As long as we get there together."

Epilogue

Roman

Two months later…

> **Talk to Me, Hothead**

"ROMAN? CAN WE TALK?" DANI QUESTIONS from my office doorway. I've long since moved into James Tucker's old office. It's only been two months since I showed him the video Brett took of Chelsea slobbing his knob, and then the other one of her admitting to getting several men at Tucker Advertising fired. He was horrified and embarrassed but not surprised. I didn't even have to remind him about my offer to purchase his company. He just told me to, "Get the ball rolling, son."

And, boy, has that ball been rolling ever since. I managed to hang on to all of the good employees and weed through any that were loyal to Chelsea, although, those were few and far between. Renaming the company and rebranding has gone well, thanks to Ram. Now that he's back in his element, he's been handling the marketing department with ease. It took some time, but I was finally able to right that wrong.

"Sure," I tell her, closing a folder in front of me. "What's up?"

She chews on her bottom lip and regards me with a frown. Her hand gestures and my eye catches on the simple diamond on her ring finger. Ram did right by her. "It's Andie."

My heart stops in my chest. Christmas Eve didn't go well. I took Ram's advice and went to talk to her. After we fucked, and man was it good, she kicked me out just like I knew she would. But I was firm and said my piece. That I liked her and wanted to explore an actual relationship besides fucking. She not so kindly told me, and I quote, "I don't *do* relationships and as of now, I no longer *do* you."

I thought she'd been kidding, but she was serious. In the past two months, I've seen her when I go out with Dani and Ram, but we haven't fucked. That much. Way less than before. Okay, so it was this morning. But still…we're in no better position than we were months ago. Hate fucking on speed dial is how you'd define our "relationship."

"What's wrong?"

"She wasn't herself this morning at the bank. I can always tell when Andie is off. She's crabbier than normal and emotional. Something has upset her. Was it you and her?"

I reflect back to this morning when she showed up at the loft on the way to work. She'd looked as though she actually wanted to talk but stupid me was in a hurry. I just tossed her over my shoulder and took her to my room.

Once I had my lips on her neck, her words died in her throat. We fucked, and then she left in a huff. Business as usual for us.

"She seemed okay. I would offer to talk to her but she hates me," I tell her.

Dani lets out a sound of frustration. "Well, she won't even talk to me right now which is a first. But that's not why I'm here. She got…well, she told off our boss…you see, she got fir—"

She's cut off when Andie storms into my office. I drag my gaze from Dani to take in the woman, who only hours ago, I had my cock sunk deep inside. When we're fucking, the chaotic world around us seems to go quiet. But the moment we come, it's game back on.

"Dani, go. I need to have a word with big boy over there," Andie snaps, causing her friend to jolt in surprise.

Dani shoots me a look that begs for me to get to the bottom of things but be nice in the process. I'm great at getting to the bottom of things. Nice…not so much. She gives me a thankful smile, squeezes Andie along the way, and then shuts the door behind her. Andie is tense as fuck and drops her purse to the floor. Her body is physically shaking. I'm out of my chair in an instant, the need to comfort her surprisingly overwhelming me. When I get close to her, she hisses.

"This is all your fault!" Her dark blonde eyebrows are furled together in an angry manner. She starts to pace, but I grab her by the elbow and haul her into my arms. Her body squirms at first, but then she sags against me in defeat. I stroke her sleek blonde hair that seems to be getting longer each day. She doesn't hug me back, but she certainly doesn't try to pull away.

"What's my fault? Talk to me, hothead."

She lets out a ragged breath, and I fear she's barely holding in tears. "I got fired."

Pulling away, I look down at her. Her pretty blue eyes shimmer with unshed tears and her plump bottom lip wobbles madly. I slide my hand to her throat and reach up with my thumb to stop it. Hot breath tickles my thumb.

"Why did you get fired?" I ask softly, my gaze fixated on her perfect mouth.

She lets out a whimper of defeat. "I was late and having a really shitty day and—"

"Aren't you always late?" I retort, smirking at her.

A half-smile tugs at her lips. "Not *this* late." She huffs. "Besides, I never told off my boss before. I'd had enough, though. I was feeling like crap. I just told him to—"

"Go fuck himself?"

At least this earns me a cute smile. Usually, I'm privy to the vicious, evil grins or the devious fuck-me-against-the-fireplace smiles. Never the adorable ones. Those, she keeps locked in a vault around me.

"He didn't like it and canned me."

"I'm sorry my big dick got you fired," I tell her with a smug grin. "But I can fix this. I happen to know the boss at this other company. He's lenient with hotties who are late because they've been busy getting the D. In fact, he's supportive of that reason." I'm trying to cheer her up, but it only pisses her off.

"I knew you'd make a joke about it. This is serious! I have…responsibilities. I can't be on the streets," she yells, jerking away from me. This time, the tears do escape, which really fucking scares me. Andie is never this upset about anything. She's mean and hateful but never sad and vulnerable.

"Come on," I growl, grabbing her by the elbow. She starts bitching at me as I drag her out of my office. We both ignore the shocked stares of everyone around us as I haul her down to Chance Douglas's office. We're going to fix this right now. As soon as I burst into his office, he stares up at me wide eyed. Then, his eyes slip over to Andie. A flicker of appreciation washes over his features before he schools them. I tamper down the jealousy and get down to business.

"Give her a job," I order.

Chance frowns at me. "As your HR person, I would first suggest you take your hand off this potential employee—"

"Not potential. Give her a job, now."

"Roman! You're being a little shit right now," she gripes, unsuccessfully trying to wriggle from my grip.

"Roman, buddy," Chance starts. "The only job open right now is—"

"Whatever it is, give it to her. Now. Make her sign the paperwork. Pay her much better than what she made at the bank," I cut in.

Chance lets out a breath of frustrated air. "Fine. Ma'am, please sit."

She gives me a scathing look before plopping down in the chair. I don't miss the relief in her shoulders, though. And that has my male pride thumping wildly in my chest. I leave the office and head back toward mine. Twenty minutes later, Andie comes strolling in my office like she owns the joint.

"You messed up, you big oaf," she tells me, her deviant smile in place. "You guys are now paying me double what I made at the bank." Pride shines in her eyes and it gets my dick hard. "And to do what? Keep up with you? Easy fucking peasy."

Wait?

What?

She beams at me. "Executive assistant to the CEO."

Fuck.

"Oh shit," I murmur under my breath.

A brief look of hurt flashes in her eyes before she schools it away. "Oh shit is right. So show me to my desk. Where will I be sitting?"

I scrub my face and stand. Outside my office is a little cubicle, but then Chance would be free to look out his window all day at her and I'm not sure I like that idea. Actually, I'm really fucking sure I don't like that idea.

"There," I point at a conference table in the corner of my office. "Your desk is there."

She frowns and walks over to it, swaying her hips along the way. Today she looks killer hot in a short skirt and knee-high boots. Working with her every day is going to be fucking impossible.

But I do love me a challenge…

"This isn't a desk. It's a table," she argues.

"So I'll buy you a desk."

"I want a computer."

"Duh."

"And, like, one of those cute stands that you can hold all your color-coded folders in."

"Umm, fine. I don't know what that is, but sure."

"Also, I want one of those really heavy paper weights so I can throw it at you when you piss me off."

I growl. "Nope."

"A Nerf gun then? A slingshot?"

Moving into her space, I inhale her sweet scent before sliding my hands to her waist. "Is that all?"

"Umm, I want two hour lunches."

"No."

"Please?"

"Only if you have lunch with me."

Silence.

She turns in my arms and surprisingly doesn't hit or kick me. "You know this is a really bad idea, right?"

I palm her ass and pull her against me so she feels how hard I am. "I'm comfortable in my choices."

Once again, her eyes shimmer with an emotion that I believe is happiness. As if, for once, I've said the right goddamned thing.

"We can't fuck here," I murmur, my lips finding the shell of her ear.

She moans and her fingers grip at the front of my suit. "Over there then?"

I laugh and steal her lips with mine. She lets me kiss her sweetly for a good thirty seconds before she starts trying to undress me.

"Andie," I groan and pull away from her. "Not here. Not right now."

Hurt flashes in her eyes before she lets anger guard her heart. "Not here. Not now. Not ever. Got it. Anything else, Mr. Holloway?" She jerks away and crosses her arms over her ample chest. *Goddamn those tits.*

"Don't be like that. I just…I want to…you and I can't…"

"I should have known better," she snaps and starts toward the door.

Frowning in confusion, I trot after her. "Should have known what?"

Her blonde hair whips around as she glares at me, her finger right in my face. "That this was all a fucking joke. I knew it. For one tiny second I thought it wasn't. Fuck me, was I wrong."

I reach for her, but the little psycho kicks me in the fucking shin. Again. I have a permanent bruise there from her.

"Fuck!" I roar.

She gives me the middle finger. "I read the tiny print on those forms. You can't fire me for pre-existing conditions. I'm your nightmare now. Since this is all your fault, you deserve it."

Confusion washes over me. "What the fuck are you talking about?"

Again, tears well in her eyes before she quickly blinks them away. "Tomorrow, I will start and I want all of my requests met."

"I already told you. Done. Now would you stop being so damn hormonal and talk to me?" I demand.

She gives me a shove and hisses like a fucking cat. "Hormonal?" she screeches, her voice shrill. "You haven't seen hormonal yet!"

"Andie—"

"I'm pregnant."

Blink. Blink. Blink.

"And it's yours. See you tomorrow, Daddy Douchebag."

Roman and Andie's story continues soon in…

Hate 2 Lovers

Dear Reader,

So you made it to the end and you want to know who wrote what...

Since J.D. Hollyfield writes fun, feisty females, we left Dani (and Andie) to her! And since K Webster loves writing a tortured male, we left Ram (and Roman) up to her!

Did you guess right?
Did you have fun?

We hope you enjoyed our little book and thank you for taking the time to post a review. *Hate 2 Lovers* will come out before you know it and we're pumped to write all about Andie and Roman—those two are crazy!

If you want to have more fun with us, come find us in our active reader groups on FB. We like popping into each other's groups and harassing each other from time to time (okay every day)! See ya there!

K & J

Acknowledgements
K WEBSTER

A huge thank you to my amazing friend J.D. Hollyfield. What started as a story about a guy named Tom and his kink for making love to frozen turkeys, we've come a long way in turning a silly concept into an actual real romance story where no headless poultry were harmed by basement dwelling hillbillies with a hard-on. One day we'll pick up Turkey Tom again though and we'll make that story our bitch. Until then, I look forward to more of these conventional type romances with you. The cuntversations we have are brilliant and I'm glad we are so cute. We really are *soooo* cute.

Thank you to my husband, Matt. I love you more than words can describe. Your support means the world.

I want to thank the people who read this beta book early and gave me incredible support. Elizabeth Clinton, Ella Stewart, Amanda Soderlund, Amy Bosica, Shannon Martin, Brooklyn Miller, Robin Martin, Amy Simms, and Sunny Borek. (I hope I didn't forget anyone.) You guys always provide AMAZING feedback. You all give me helpful ideas to make my stories better and give me incredible encouragement. I appreciate all of your comments and suggestions. Love you ladies!

Also, a big thank you to Vanessa Renee Place for

proofreading our story after editing. You always save me in a pinch and I can't thank you enough!! Love ya!

A big thank you to my author friends who have given me your friendship and your support. You have no idea how much that means to me.

Thank you to all of my blogger friends both big and small that go above and beyond to always share my stuff. You all rock! #AllBlogsMatter

I'm especially thankful for my Krazy for K Webster's Books reader group. You ladies are wonderful with your support and friendship. Each and every single one of you is amazingly supportive and caring. #Cucumbers4Life

I am totally thankful for my author group, the COPA gals, for being there when I need to take a load off and whine. Y'all rock!

Vanessa Bridges and Manda Lee from Prema Editing, thanks so much for editing our book!
Thank you Stacey Blake for working through a time crunch and always being so flexible. I love you! I love you! I love you!

A big thanks to my PR gal, Nicole Blanchard. You are fabulous at what you do and keep me on track! And also thank you to The Hype PR gals for sharing the love!

Lastly but certainly not least of all, thank you to all of

the wonderful readers out there that are willing to hear my story and enjoy my characters like I do. It means the world to me!

Acknowledgements
J.D. HOLLYFIELD

Thank you first to my bomb ass husband. Who always puts me before himself. I know it takes a lot to deal with a writer. So thank you for all those times you've questioned my sanity at two in the morning, and just turned and walked away. Since they haven't invented a word strong enough for how much I love you so we will stick with the four letter word for now.

To K. Webster, who I think is an okay gal and probably wouldn't jump in front of a bus for, but definitely would whistle to warn her or something. Thank you for being awesome and funny and scary all in one. This friendship has been one big laugh after another. You are talented and kind and one giving human. My heart feels funny just knowing I have such an amazing friend in my life and I cunt believe how lucky I am. I'm thankful for you. And always remember, "We're so cute."

Thank you to my editor Vanessa Bridges and her team at PREMA for their efforts in this story. Thank you to my amazing Beta team, and all the ladies who offered their eyes on this project. Amy Wiater, Jennifer Hanson, and anyone else I missed who took the time to jump on my story and work together to make it what it is today. I appreciate you all!

Thank you to All by Design for the amazing cover! You nailed it. As you nail everything else. (Not everyone. Whole nother conversation…)

Thank you to my awesome reader group, Club JD. All your constant support for what I do warms my heart. I appreciate all the time you take in helping my stories come to life within this community.

A big hug and wine clink to Stacey at Champagne Formats for always making my books look so pretty.

And most importantly every single reader and blogger! THANK YOU for all that you do. For supporting me, reading my stories, spreading the word. It's because of you that I get to continue in this business. And for that I am forever grateful.

Cheers. This big glass of wine is for you.

K WEBSTER

K Webster is the author of dozens of romance books in many different genres including contemporary romance, historical romance, paranormal romance, dark romance, romantic suspense, and erotic romance. When not spending time with her husband of nearly fourteen years and two adorable children, she's active on social media connecting with her readers.

Her other passions besides writing include reading and graphic design. K can always be found in front of her computer chasing her next idea and taking action. She looks forward to the day when she will see one of her titles on the big screen.

Join K Webster's newsletter to receive a couple of updates a month on new releases and exclusive content. To join, all you need to do is go here (www.authorkwebster.com).

Facebook: www.facebook.com/authorkwebster

Blog: authorkwebster.wordpress.com

Twitter: twitter.com/KristiWebster

Email: kristi@authorkwebster.com

Goodreads:
www.goodreads.com/user/show/10439773-k-webster

Instagram: instagram.com/kristiwebster

Books by
K WEBSTER

The Breaking the Rules Series:
Broken (Book 1)
Wrong (Book 2)
Scarred (Book 3)
Mistake (Book 4)
Crushed (Book 5 – a novella)

The Vegas Aces Series:
Rock Country (Book 1)
Rock Heart (Book 2)
Rock Bottom (Book 3)

The Becoming Her Series:
Becoming Lady Thomas (Book 1)
Becoming Countess Dumont (Book 2)
Becoming Mrs. Benedict (Book 3)

Alpha & Omega Duet:
Alpha & Omega
Omega & Love

War & Peace Duet
This is War, Baby
This is Love, Baby
This Isn't Over, Baby
This Isn't You, Baby

Standalone Novels

Apartment 2B
Love and Law
Moth to a Flame
Erased
The Road Back to Us
Give Me Yesterday
Running Free
Dirty Ugly Toy (Dark Romance)
Zeke's Eden
Sweet Jayne
Untimely You
Mad Sea
Pretty Stolen Dolls
Pretty Lost Dolls
Whispers and the Roars
Schooled by a Senior
Blue Hill Blood by Elizabeth Gray

About
J.D. HOLLYFIELD

Creative designer, mother, wife, writer, part time superhero...

J.D. Hollyfield is a creative designer by day and superhero by night. When she is not trying to save the world one happy ending at a time, she enjoys the snuggles of her husband, son and three doxies. With her love for romance, and head full of book boyfriends, she was inspired to test her creative abilities and bring her own story to life.

J.D. Hollyfield lives in the Midwest, and is currently at work on blowing the minds of readers, with the additions of her new books and series, along with her charm, humor and HEA's.

Read MORE of J.D. Hollyfield

My So Called Life:
Life Next Door
Life in a Rut, Love not Included
Life as we Know it
Faking It
Unlocking Adeline
Sinful Instincts
Passing Peter Parker

CONNECT WITH J.D. Hollyfield

Website: authorjdhollyfield.com

Facebook: www.facebook.com/authorjdhollyfield

Twitter: twitter.com/jdhollyfield

Newsletter: http://eepurl.com/Wf7gv

Pinterest: www.pinterest.com/jholla311/

Instagram: instagram.com/jdhollyfield

Made in the USA
Las Vegas, NV
29 April 2023

71291989R00154